For my good
friend Jim

LION

AT

TWILIGHT

Roger.

ROGER L. CONLEE

Pale Horse Books

ISBN: 978-1-939917-26-3

Cover Design: Mark A. Clements

ALSO by Roger L. Conlee:

EVERY SHAPE, EVERY SHADOW
COUNTERCLOCKWISE
THE HINDENBURG LETTER
SOULS ON THE WIND
DARE THE DEVIL
DEEP WATER
AFTER THE WIND

www.PaleHorseBooks.com
www.RogerLConlee.com

For Jim Nelson,
great friend and bookworm

LION
AT
TWILIGHT

ROGER L. CONLEE

A JAKE & ILSE WEAVER
NOVEL

ONE

September 1953

"The Prime Minister has been kidnapped," said the voice on the phone.

"Winston Churchill?" said Jake Weaver, the West Coast correspondent for CBS News.

"We believe so." Jake recognized the voice. It belonged to Colonel Harold Freeborn, a retired operative for Britain's MI6, a man who'd had many close dealings with Jake during World War II.

Jake was seated in a red leatherette booth at Musso & Frank's, a popular eatery on Hollywood Boulevard, across from mobster Mickey Cohen, a news source and arm's-length friend of his. An elderly waiter had brought the phone to the booth and plugged it into an outlet, saying "You have a call, Mr. Weaver."

"It happened in Berlin," Freeborn explained, the transatlantic call surprisingly clear. "Sir Winston was on a state visit to the Federal Republic of Germany, West Germany's official name, to confer with Chancellor Adenauer. You doubtless heard about it. Then he decided to go to divided Berlin to call on West Berlin's mayor, and there he simply disappeared. We've had no word from him for two days. So far we've kept this from the newspapers, but that could change at any moment. We're frightfully concerned."

Was old Winston really missing or was he up to something? Jake wondered. Churchill had always been an adventurer. He'd been taken prisoner and then escaped during the Boer War in South Africa, and had been at the front with the Royal Scots Fusiliers during World War I. He'd coined the term "the Iron Curtain" in 1946. What could possibly have happened in Berlin to the old lion, now 79 years old?

"Have you had a call demanding ransom," Jake asked, "anything like that?"

"Nothing. Nary a word."

"I understand your concern, but what's this got to do with me, sir?"

"Jake, you must call me Harold. We're old friends. You know Berlin. You were there during the war, at great personal risk, and you're a splendid sleuth. Even got the rocket man von Braun into our care. We're hoping you could lend us a hand."

"I'll have to give that some thought. But you're retired, sir, er, Harold. Why are you involved in this?"

"Ha. MI6 never lets one get too far away. Please say you'll go."

Jake was already pretty sure he would. His wife Valerie wouldn't like it, but CBS would. This could be a big story. He asked a few more questions, took down

Freeborn's number and said he'd get back to him ASAP. MI6 was Britain's foreign intelligence service, much older and more experienced than America's CIA.

After ringing off with Freeborn, Mickey Cohen gave Jake a look and said, "What was that all about, Jakester?" *

Jake had been working on a possible story about crime in San Diego and its top underworld figure, Frank Bompensiero. Cohen had dropped a hint or two about the man.

When Jake explained about the call, Cohen said, "You should go, pal. This kinda stuff is right up your alley."

Mickey Cohen was L.A.'s top mobster. He'd eclipsed his principal rival, Jack Dragna, and was on good terms with the Mafia in New York and Chicago. Jake sometimes got good inside information from the man.

They finished up their rich chicken pot pies, for which Musso's was famous, their glasses of Scotch, and departed with Cohen saying," See you in church, kid," his favorite parting line.

On the drive to his home on Saturn Avenue, Jake reflected that Winston Churchill had shockingly been voted out of office in 1945 after being the wartime face and symbol of British resolve, but was called back to the PM post in 1951 after the Labour Party failed to deliver the vast postwar social reforms it had promised.

Well, the whole thing could be over and done with

by the time Jake could get there. It could take two or three days to reach Berlin, flying to New York, London, Frankfurt, and finally Tempelhof Field in Berlin. He'd have to get approval from CBS, not to mention Valerie, which could be tougher.

Jake thought about his wife, who worked in rocket design at Lockheed, one of the few women in the U.S. in that field. They'd been married for eleven years. Valerie had been worried to death when he'd sneaked into Nazi Germany during the war, twice, running dangerous errands for President Roosevelt as well as MI6. She wouldn't like this at all.

What Valerie saw in him Jake didn't know. She was a tall, willowy brunette with vivid blue eyes while he, only one inch taller, had reddish to rusty brown hair that was starting to recede, and a ruddy complexion on a face that had been hit too often in a brief amateur boxing career. But she loved him. Go figure.

Reaching home, he parked in the driveway, entered their Craftsman-style home, and found his daughter Ilse there. A 23-year-old reporter for the Pasadena *Star-News*, she'd come over to have dinner with her father and stepmother. Ilse had been born in Germany in 1930, had lived there during the Depression and early war years, and come to the U.S. in 1942. Her English was perfect but still spoken with a trace of accent.

Jake had been in Germany in 1930 for a memorial service for his Aunt Marta and, single at the time, had enjoyed a brief affair with an attractive German woman.

Hence, Ilse.

Father and daughter sometimes reminisced on how her mother, Winifrid, had kept her pregnancy secret and that Jake knew nothing of Ilse till they'd met in 1942 when he'd sneaked into Nazi Berlin with the help of MI6. They managed to flee Germany together through Sweden.

In the kitchen, Jake greeted his women with hugs and kisses, noting again that Ilse's brown eyes and reddish hair were much like his own.

"Welcome home, Sailor," Valerie said. "How was your day?" She often called him Sailor, knowing he'd been in the Navy in the '30s before starting his journalism career. Not waiting for Jake's reply, she said, "Dinner's in about an hour so let's relax and have some wine in the front room."

Valerie and Ilse settled on the sofa and Jake took a seat on an easy chair facing them, wine goblets and an already opened bottle of zinfandel on the coffee table between them. Aha, the gals had a head start.

Ilse said "Cheers" as they clinked glasses and then told of a story she was working on for the *Star-News*: renovations at the Tournament of Roses building on Colorado Boulevard. She had been editor of the *Daily Bruin* at UCLA before graduating and taking the Pasadena job.

Valerie described some exciting new pictures from near space that were taken from the Viking 11 rocket she'd worked on.

Ilse then asked, "And what did you do today, *Vati*? To Jake's delight she still called him by the German word for daddy.

Jake had been a newspaper reporter and editor for years but quit the *Herald-Express* after the death of William Randolph Hearst. He didn't get along with Hearst's son when he took over as publisher. He'd accepted an offer from CBS.

He described a story he was working on about the faux pro wrestling that was popular on local TV. Interviews he'd had with hulks describing themselves as Gorgeous George and the Argentine Backbreaker. He also mentioned the San Diego story he'd been quizzing Mickey Cohen about.

Ilse said, "Maybe I should change the spelling of my name to Ilsa, with an 'a'. Some people mispronounce it, calling me 'Aisle' or 'Izzly' or some such."

"No," Jake replied. "Be proud of your birth name."

"Absolutely right," Valerie put in.

That settled, Jake finally got around to the call from Colonel Freeborn about Winston Churchill's disappearance and asking for his help. He mentally braced himself for Valerie's objection.

But she said, "I'm not thrilled about you going to Germany for the third time in ten years, but I think you should. It'd be a big story and would help your career."

Whew! Before Jake could say how glad he was to hear that, Ilse jumped in with, "I'd love to see my hometown again. I have some vacation coming up. I'm going with you, *Vati*!"

TWO

Though surprised, Jake liked the sound of that. Ilse knew Berlin even better than he did, and two heads are better than one, the saying goes. When Valerie demurred, saying it would be dangerous for her stepdaughter, Jake raised those points, and Ilse enthusiastically added some of her own.

What Berlin was like these days was the main topic of conversation over a dinner of lamb chops, steamed broccoli, and a green salad. Jake pointed out that the Western Allies had controlled West Berlin until two years ago and that now it was basically a free city regarded as a West German state, even though it was isolated deep within East Germany. East Berlin was a communist municipality under the thumb of the Kremlin.

U.S. and British troops remained in West Berlin as an occupation and protective force.

Each zone had its own mayor and city hall. People could travel between the two, the trams and subways still operating, but it was growing more difficult. Since a massive workers' strike this year, the East Berlin cops, known as the People's Police or *Stasi*, were stopping and hassling legitimate commuters, even those who had jobs in the opposite sector.

"I've heard about the manpower drain," Ilse said, "that teachers and technicians have been fleeing to the western zone because conditions are so much better there."

"Right," Jake replied, "and the west is doing a lot of rebuilding from bomb damage, helped by some U.S. aid. The Reds don't seem to care so much. Walt Cronkite did a story for us on that a while back."

"I wonder if my old school is still standing," Ilse said.

After dinner, the three returned to the front room with small bowls of chocolate ice cream.

"What's your next step, *Vati*?" Ilse asked.

"I'll call CBS in New York in the morning, *Liebchen*, and see what they say. If I get the green light I'll have to tell Freeborn I want you to come with me. Don't put in for vacation till I get his okay. So, we've got some hurdles to jump before we can hop on a plane. I'll call you at the paper as soon as I can, hopefully in the morning."

"And tonight you'll probably toss and turn and I won't get any sleep," Valerie said.

"Yeah, maybe I should bed down in the spare room," Jake replied.

"No way, big guy, no way," Valerie said with what he called The Look.

Ilse blushed.

* * *

After a satisfying roll in the hay for him and Valerie—she'd said "I needed that, Sailor"—Jake had trouble getting to sleep. Questions swirled. Did President Eisenhower know about this? Did the CIA? West German intelligence? Above all, if Churchill really had been kidnapped, who was behind it? It couldn't have been Joseph Stalin—he was five months dead. Jake didn't know much about the new Soviet premier, Georgi Malenkov.

At last he drifted into sleep, and in one of his dreams he was walking along Unter den Linden in East Berlin where black, red and yellow East German flags fluttered from buildings along with the red hammer and sickle pennants of the USSR.

At 6 a.m., feeling anything but rested, he slipped out of bed, put on a pot of coffee, and called Douglas Edwards, the managing editor of CBS Television News. It would be 9 o'clock in New York.

Instantly seeing this as a big story, Edwards agreed that he should go.

"Great," Jake said, "but Doug, can I ask you to keep the lid on this for now? MI6 wants to keep it quiet as long as possible."

"I think so."

"You'd better *know* so. Breaking it now could blow the rapport I have with MI6."

"I believe we can do that," Edwards said.

"Believe it strongly, Doug. Okay then, I'll call the Brits and say I'm in. Thanks."

Valerie came into the kitchen at that moment, rubbing sleep from her eyes, and poured two cups of coffee. She kissed him on the cheek and said with smiling eyes, "Sure glad you didn't sleep in the spare room last night." She sipped some coffee and added, "So what did the brass in New York say?"

"Gave me the go-ahead, sweetie. Now I'll call Freeborn—oughta be a little after 3 p.m. in London."

"Reverse the charges, big guy."

Jake laughed and said he would.

It took about four minutes for the transatlantic call to go through, but at last he reached the colonel.

"Good man. I knew we could count on you," Freeborn said.

"Is there anything new today?" Jake asked. "Any further word on the prime minister?"

"No, nothing, I'm sorry to say."

Jake then said he'd like to bring Ilse along.

"Oh yes, your daughter. Born in Berlin, wasn't she? I suppose that will be all right. Her knowledge of the city could be useful. Fly to Washington on one of your domestic airlines, then we'll whisk you to London from Bolling Air Force Base on one of our new military jets. We'll cover your travel expenses, of course, but not the Los Angeles to Washington flight for the young lady. I hope you understand."

Jake said he did. He knew postwar Britain was basically broke.

"Leave as soon as possible, Jake."

"We'll be in the air tomorrow, sir." *I hope.*

After he hung up, Valerie said, "I think I spoke too soon yesterday when I said you should go."

Oh oh. Valerie rarely stood in his way. She'd been extremely worried both times he went into Nazi Germany during the war but hadn't put her foot down. What now?

"I've been doing some rethinking," she said. "I know there's no stopping you when your mind is made up. Determination is one of your best qualities. And I understand Ilse wanting to see her hometown again, but there's something about this that bothers me. I can't quite put my finger on it."

"You've always had good instincts, Val, but—"

"Why can't British agents handle this?" she interrupted. "They're trained in this kind of thing."

"I guess Colonel Freeborn regards me as some kind of super amateur since I found Wernher von Braun when his men couldn't."

"The rocket guy?"

"Right, the rocket guy. You know, Val, I was more scared on Guadalcanal than either time I was in Hitler's Germany. The night those Jap battleships blasted hell out of the U.S. base I thought I was a goner. Really believed I was gonna die. I don't see much danger here at all."

Valerie put a hand on his arm and said, "I hope you're right, Sailor. I won't try to stop you even if I could."

THREE

It took a day for them to get everything arranged. Ilse said she had a little trouble with her managing editor over getting her vacation started immediately. She had a couple of assignments on her plate.

"I hope you didn't jeopardize your job," Jake said.

"No, I don't think so. I've been a very good reporter for them."

Jake booked a flight to Washington on TWA that would include a stopover at Midway Airport in Chicago. This first leg of their journey would take hours.

One last call from Colonel Freeborn related that they'd be briefed at MI6 in London, given whatever new information they might have, further instructions, and flown to Berlin the same day.

Valerie went all out and prepared a lush dinner for their last night together. Leg of lamb, sautéed mushrooms, baked potatoes, and salad. Jake popped open a bottle of Napa pinot noir. They reminisced about the good times they'd had in eleven years of marriage.

Jake was glad to see Valerie giving him The Look before going to bed.

* * *

The next morning, she drove them to what had been renamed Los Angeles International Airport from the original Mines Field. In front of the terminal building, she told Ilse, "Take care of the old guy now. I'm always saying he damn well better come back to me and once again he'd damn well better." She hugged them both and gave Jake a lingering kiss. "I'm sorry I spoke up last night," she said. "Please take good care of yourself."

"Always, sweetie."

Jake and Ilse hiked up the portable stairway and took their seats. Soon the sleek, silvery Lockheed Constellation took off, climbed to the west over Dockweiler Beach, made a slow southward turn over white swells dancing in the Pacific, and began to angle back over the L.A. basin.

Jake heard the baritone drone of the four Wright Cyclone engines. He looked down and glimpsed the Hollywood Sign over the Santa Monica Mountains, which minutes later gave way to the San Gabriels and San Bernardinos. The plane soared over the Mount Baldy and San Gorgonio peaks, then the desert beyond. Down below, the steel tracks of the Southern Pacific etched a long silvery line across the dry flatlands as if drawn by hand.

"Well, *Liebchen*," Jake said, "We're on our way."

"Right, *Vati*, I'm excited. Maybe I'll be able to see *Grossonkel* Dieter,"she said," using the German for great uncle. The retired Berlin policeman would be about 70 now. He had great contacts there and could possibly be of help.

Jake's thoughts turned to his friend Kenny Nielsen in San Diego. The retired Marine Corps colonel was now a high school history teacher and his wife Claudia, a physician, had opened her medical practice there.

Jake knew Kenny had been having a lot of bad dreams about his horrific experiences at Guadalcanal, Pelelieu, and Okinawa during World War II and later at the Chosin Reservoir in North Korea. He'd said the faces of enemy soldiers he'd killed often appeared in his sleep. Jake hoped that would soon fade away, that his postwar traumas would become a thing of the past.

He empathized. Jake had killed three Germans himself during the war. All in self-defense. It had been his life or theirs. Those jagged moments often haunted him.

Ilse took a sip of coffee and said, "I hope Claudia and Kenny are doing okay, that her doctor practice is off to a good start and that Kenny's healing." She and Claudia had shared an apartment during their last year at UCLA.

"Me too," Jake said. "Let's go down and see them after we get back."

They each read a bit as the hours passed. Jake had brought along William Shirer's book *Berlin Diary* and *The Long Goodbye* by his friend Raymond Chandler. Ilse had several magazines, including *Collier's* and *Life*.

Pushing one of them aside, Ilse said, "I know

Churchill was respected for rallying the British against Hitler, making defiant speeches and all that, but what else can you tell me about him?"

"One reason I like the man, *Liebchen*, is that he started out as a news reporter, just like us. In 1899 he was covering the Boer War in South Africa for the *Daily Mail* when he got captured. Somehow he managed to escape and make it 200 miles back to British lines. This made him an instant national hero. In World War I he was First Lord of the Admiralty when he planned an amphibious landing behind Turkish lines to capture Istanbul. It failed miserably, so he resigned in disgrace and went off to serve in the front lines in France. He was in Parliament between the wars where he warned that Hitler was a menace and Britain should rearm."

"That's when I was in the BDM," Ilse said, referring to the *Bund Deutscher Maidel*, the girls' section of the Hitler Youth. "I was taught that Hitler was almost a god and I believed them. How dumb I was."

"You weren't dumb, not at all, just young and impressionable. Your eyes hadn't been opened yet. Anyway, Churchill became prime minister on the worst possible day in 1940, the day the Germans broke through in the Ardennes and began their race to the sea, which trapped the Brits at Dunkirk."

"Okay, that part I know, *Vati*, how they evacuated by sea and he made his 'tears, blood and sweat' speech. He was quite a man, then. What a life he had."

"So true, Ilse, and let's pray that life is not over."

* * *

There was a forty-minute stop at Midway Airport to refuel and change passengers. When Jake and Ilse deplaned to stretch their legs for a few minutes, some light sprinkles drifted down on them from a slate-gray sky. Jake thought about going inside to call his friend Bill Stoneman of the *Chicago Daily News*, but decided not to. Stoneman would want to know what he was doing in Chicago and where he was headed, and Jake didn't care to explain. Nor would MI6 want him to.

The trek resumed and somewhere over Ohio a pretty, flaxen-haired stewardess stopped by and asked, "Are you two going to see all the sights in Washington?"

"Not this time," Jake said. "We'll just be passing through on our way to London and Berlin."

"Berlin? Gee sir, that could be dangerous for you, those communist troops and all."

"Dangerous? Not a bit," Jake fibbed. *Yeah, it could be.*

FOUR

The plane touched down at Washington National Airport in Arlington, Virginia at 7:30 p.m. Eastern Daylight Time.

Jake and Ilse collected their bags from the overhead bin and climbed down. Just inside the terminal they sighted a man holding a cardboard sign saying WEAVER. He showed his British ID and said he was Agent Backus. "Come with me, please, we have a car waiting."

Soon Jake and Ilse were seated in the back of a black Packard Clipper four-door. As they were driven south down the George Washington Parkway, Ilse saw in the distance the lighted Capitol Building and Washington Monument. "They look even nicer in person than in pictures," she exclaimed. "The capital of my new adopted country! I'd love to come back here someday and give it a good looking-over."

They reached the Woodrow Wilson Bridge, crossed the Potomac, and drove up the east side of the river to Bolling Air Force Base. Agent Backus showed his ID at the guard post and they drove in the dark past several barracks and hangars, eventually arriving at the flight line where a sleek British fighter-bomber stood on a taxiway.

Backus wished Jake and Ilse good luck and told them to board. Jake said, "Thanks, fella," and shook the man's hand.

He and Ilse collected their bags and climbed the portable stairway, where a three-man crew waited at the top. The pilot introduced himself, the copilot, and navigator. "Welcome," he said. "This is a Canberra B-2. Two Rolls-Royce Avon turbojets, fast and reliable. We'll get you to old Blighty in about seven hours. We have rather small quarters for you, I'm afraid." He motioned them to a space behind the navigator's bench. No seats. "You'll have to bunk down there over the bomb bay. Not to worry, those bomb doors are tightly secured."

Jake laughed and said he sure as heck hoped so. The pilot grinned at that and said, "We have some sandwiches and a Thermos of coffee for you. Some blankets as well."

Jake and Ilse crawled in. He surveyed the space and suggested they sit up against the fuselage, arranging blankets behind them so they could sit in at least some semi-comfort.

The navigator leaned back from his perch in front of them and said, "It's not exactly the Savoy, is it? Best we can do for you, though. Let me know if you need anything."

Ilse thanked him and soon the two engines roared to

life. After a minute the pilot called out, "We're cleared for takeoff. Are you ready back there?"

Jake said, "All set, Lieutenant," and the plane taxied to the head of the runway, stopped there a moment, and then bolted down it. Jake put a hand on an aluminum rib to steady himself as the thrust of acceleration threw him a little off balance. Ilse did the same. The takeoff and climb-out was fast. Jake found the soprano pitch of the engines much different than the drone of the propeller-driven planes he was used to.

"I'm disappointed I can't look out and see lights of Washington," he said. "First time I've ridden on a jet, Ilse. It's quite an experience."

"It sure is, *Vati.*"

When the plane leveled off, Ilse picked up the Thermos and poured coffee into two pasteboard cups.

After taking a sip, she said, "A few hours ago we were over the Pacific and now in the very same day, we'll soon be over the Atlantic. Pretty *verlunderwich.* I prefer the German word for amazing."

"It's *verlunderwich* for sure," Jake agreed. He drank some coffee. Too much cream for his taste but what the hell.

Later they opened a box of sandwiches. Jake unwrapped one and said with a frown, "Cucumbers and cheese. I'd prefer ham or turkey, but beggars can't be choosers." All the while he heard the crew conversing, discussing their course, fuel consumption, and such.

The food unenthusiastically consumed, they settled down for the long flight and fell into some father-daughter conversation. Jake, who'd had years of newspaper experience, asked how Ilse liked the *Star-News*. And was she dating anyone? The answers were fine and sort-of, but not seriously. She asked about the differences between newspaper work and TV news. The reporting was pretty much the same but some other jobs were unique, like that of producer. And of course they pondered what they might be able to do to find Winston Churchill.

"Whatever could have happened to the man?" Ilse wondered.

"I don't know but there's something fishy about all this. Maybe we'll be able to figure it out, possibly with Uncle Dieter's help."

"*Vater*, I have a confession to make," Ilse suddenly said. She rarely called him by the more formal father. "My managing editor didn't approve early vacation for me so I guess I'm AWOL, as they say in the military."

"Oh Ilse, it hurts to hear you say that. It's all my fault for getting you excited about this."

"Definitely not, *Vati*. Don't blame yourself. Isn't it the kind of rogue stunt you yourself sometimes undertook in your newspaper days?"

"You've got me there, *Leibchen*."

"Don't worry about me," Ilse said. "If I lose my job I can always get another. I'm going to be the next Nellie Bly."

Jake knew about Nellie Bly, but was surprised his

daughter did. The intrepid reporter for the *New York World* had let herself be committed to an insane asylum so she could expose the hideous conditions there. And she had traveled around the world in fewer than eighty days to break the famous record set by Jules Verne's fictitious Phileas Fogg.

"The next Nellie Bly, huh?" Jake said. "She was probably the most famous woman in American journalism. And why not? You've got the brains and the spunk."

"Inherited from you, *Vati*." Said with a broad smile.

Fatigue finally set in and they rearranged the blankets and bedded down for a little shuteye. Jake used his satchel as a pillow. He tried to forget he was directly over the bomb bay doors. An accidental touch of a switch could probably open them and plunge them into a black eternity.

A few hours later he was dreaming—nightmaring really—about being fired on by a German night fighter when he was aboard a Halifax heavy bomber. He could hear the staccato chatter of machine-gun fire. This had actually happened to him in 1942.

Other memories of moments in his life intruded on half-sleep as the plane droned onward. His amateur boxing days in the Navy in the '30s. The great left hook he once had. The joy when he'd outpointed Buster Grimes in twelve rounds to win the middleweight championship of the 6th Naval District. The swollen cheekbone that went along with the trophy.

Meeting and falling for Dixie Freitas, a cocktail

waitress in Longview, Texas, when he'd been a rookie reporter with the *Evening Journal*. Dixie said Jake, who was born in Louisiana, still had a lot of "Loozanna" in his voice. Marrying Dixie, then divorcing five months later when they both realized they'd made a big mistake.

Surviving a plane crash north of Oceanside when he and Vern Hatfield had been trying to fly to Tijuana.

Meeting Valerie Riskin at the Inglewood hospital in 1942 and realizing she was The One. His years with the *Herald-Express*, his friendships with the great city editor Aggie Underwood, fellow reporter Marko Janicek, and Shaker, his favorite bartender. Getting knocked cuckoo by pro boxer Elmer Beltz when they were sparring at the Main Street Gym.

The pilot's voice woke him from this reverie: "Care to come up here and see the sunrise over the Irish Sea?" He and Ilse did, threading their way past the navigator. Clouds glowed pink in a soft dawn sky. "Lovely," Ilse said.

Thirty minutes later they landed at RAF Base Biggin Hill where a British staff car waited to take them into London. Jake shook hands with the crew and said, "Thanks for the ride, fellas." As they drove toward the city, Ilse exclaimed, "Look how green the countryside is. It reminds me a little of Germany. Southern California is so dry and brown."

"We live in a semi-desert, *Liebchen*, with imported water."

Ilse gazed wide-eyed at all the sights when they reached the city. "So that's the famous Big Ben," she said, taking in the stately clock tower beside the Houses of Parliament. "Why do they call it that?"

"It was named after Sir Benjamin Hall, commissioner of works in the 19th century," the driver explained. "The clockface was blacked out during the war but Big Ben never failed to chime throughout the whole Blitz," he added with pride.

Black taxis and red, double-decker buses thronged the streets as they threaded their way through town, and bomb damage scarred several of the buildings they passed. Scaffolding indicated repairs being made on many of them.

Eventually they arrived at MI6 headquarters in Vauxhall Cross. Two starchy stiff Royal Marines in white gloves, green berets, and tan uniforms flanked the entrance to the cream-colored, three-tiered building on the south embankment of the Thames. As Jake and Ilse got out and approached, a slender, thirtyish man in a gray suit and wearing a black homburg came out the door. He stepped up to Jake and said, "You're Weaver, the American chap old Freeborn told us about?" The only notice he seemed to take of Ilse was a small grimace.

"That's me," Jake said.

"Terribly sorry, but you won't be needed on this. Bit of an inconvenience for you, wot?"

FIVE

Tired and upset, his diurnal clock thrown off kilter by a day and a half of travel, Jake demanded, "Whatta you mean not needed, pardner? And who the hell are you?"

"I am . . ." he began but the sudden appearance of Colonel Freeborn stopped him. The lanky old colonel had just come down the front steps.

"Bad form, Waterman, dreadfully bad form," Freeborn snapped. "Hello there, Jake, and this must be your lovely daughter." He stepped forward and took Ilse's hand. "It's grand to meet you, Miss Weaver." Ilse blushed and gave a small head bob.

Turning back to the first man, Freeborn said, "I'll sort this out, Waterman. You may leave now."

"Sir, you no longer have official status here."

"I said you may *leave!*" Freeborn sounding like a field marshal—or a drill sergeant. As Waterman winced and shuffled away, the colonel said, "I apologize for that young fool. Come with me, the both of you. You must be famished."

He led Jake and Ilse inside and down a long corridor, finally arriving at a cafeteria. "We'll chat over breakfast," he said.

The three took trays and walked along the food line. "Bangers and mash, what?" Freeborn said when he saw the Americans piling sausages and mashed potatoes on their plates. Eggs and toast, too. He selected a cup of tea while his guests helped themselves to coffee.

Soon seated at a table, Freeborn asked about their flight and how Ilse was finding life in the U.S. "You've become an American citizen, I presume?"

"Oh yes, sir, seven years ago."

When these pleasantries were out of the way, Freeborn said, "Now then, it's frightfully embarrassing for me but let me explain what's happened. Last night, Sir Anthony Eden had a brainstorm. The deputy prime minister ruled that this search for Winston must be an exclusively British operation. He thought we could better keep it quiet that way. He said absolutely no help from Americans or Canadians."

Jake knew about Anthony Eden. He'd always considered the prissy career diplomat a stuffed shirt, not in Churchill's class. "That sounds really paranoid," he said. "I gave you my word we'd keep the lid on this, and we will, plus I don't know of any Canadians being brought in."

"None have been, Jake, and I know you would honor your word. Perhaps Eden *is* being paranoid about this, but after all he is in charge of the country until this is sorted out." Freeborn raised his hands, palms forward, and said, "I am powerless in this matter and most embarrassed, as I've said. Agent Waterman never should have confronted you as he did. Asinine cock-up. Rest assured, I will see that you are flown back to Los Angeles at our expense."

Jake tossed a fork down on the table with a clang. "Thanks, but I'm not quitting. We're not British subjects. Eden can't force us not to go. So we'll go to Germany—if we can. I'll need to call CBS on that." Shifting his gaze to his daughter: "But Ilse, you can go back if you want."

Ilse made a fist. "No way, *Vati*, I'm sticking here with you."

Fiddling with a muffin, Freeborn said, "I suspected you two might see it that way. Right then, you may use my phone to call your network. I still have an office here."

"That's swell, Colonel, er, Harold," Jake replied. "I hope our doing this won't get you into trouble."

Freeborn laughed. "Trouble? What can they do? Make me retire? Already been done. And I shall not divulge that you're going on, that is, if you do. That would be my secret."

"That's great, Harold. Now is there anything else you can tell us about this situation?"

"Nothing much, I'm afraid. The West Berlin police say they are pressing their investigation assiduously. And there's still no call seeking a ransom, et cetera."

Freeborn sipped some tea, put his cup down, and continued. "But Jake, I do have a theory. You've likely heard that Sir Winston had a stroke early this year. He's fairly well recovered now but it has slowed him down a bit. The man is nearly 80 after all. There's a noted neurology specialist in West Berlin. This is only my conjecture, of course, but I suspect Churchill wanted to consult him, that he went to West Berlin actually more to see this specialist than to visit the mayor there."

"Sounds plausible," Jake said. "If I get the go-ahead from CBS, I'll want this doctor's name."

"Of course. I have also heard, although it's just a rumor," Freeborn said, "that he had something in mind that had to do with the isle of Jersey. The Channel Islands, just off Normandy, constitute the only British soil occupied by the Germans during the war."

After breakfast, the colonel led them upstairs to his office, which was smaller than his previous one, windowless and with about half the space. Well, Jake thought, he *is* retired. Many retirees would have none at all. That he had this room attested to his status from long years of high-level service. A picture of an elegant, gray-haired woman, obviously his wife, sat on the desk and another of the young Queen Elizabeth II hung from a wall.

"There's the phone," Freeborn said. "Shall Ilse and I leave and give you privacy while you make your call?"

"No need for that."

The colonel lifted the receiver and asked someone named Doris to connect him to an overseas operator.

He listened a moment, then handed it to Jake, who gave the number for CBS News in New York. While a minute of scratchy, staticky sounds filled the wire, Jake suddenly remembered, *Jesus, it's 2 or 3 a.m. back there.*

When an operator answered, he identified himself and asked if the call could be patched through to Douglas Edwards' home. Soon he was hearing a grouchy voice: "Yeah? What time is it anyway? Is the Empire State Building on fire?"

"It's Jake Weaver, Doug. Sure sorry to roust you at this hour but I just had a big curve thrown at me here in London. Here's the deal."

After the "deal" was explained, Edwards said, "I haven't got the smack to green-light you going on your own, though I would if I could. This'll have to go upstairs to Fred"—Fred Friendly was the top boss of CBS News—"or maybe even Mr. Paley himself." Meaning William Paley, the network president. "And I'm sure as hell not calling Friendly in the middle of the night. Where can I reach you in six or seven hours?"

"Uh, let me see," Jake said, "ah, at the Dorchester Hotel." *Hope we can get a room there.*

"Okay, Jake, I'll go to bat for you on this but don't hold your breath. Now let a guy go back to sleep. So long."

Jake hung up and Freeborn took the phone, jiggled the disconnect button twice, and said, "Doris, be a lamb and see if you can get a reservation for our Mr. Weaver and his daughter at the Dorchester."

He hung up and said he'd come over to the hotel and have dinner with them that evening. Then to Jake: "I know that you and your colleague Colonel Nielsen wrote a book about the war. I've read it, of course. It's quite good. Before you go off to your hotel to await your call, there's a chap I'd like you two to meet. He's not one of ours at MI6, more like a first cousin—he was with Naval Intelligence. He's written a book as well, what one calls a spy thriller. You'll have much in common, much to talk about. His name is Ian Fleming."

SIX

Ninety minutes later, Colonel Freeborn introduced Jake and Ilse to Ian Fleming in a small conference room at MI6. Jake took note of the man's thin brown hair, a high forehead, and that he looked to be in his mid-forties. His handshake was firm, his smile friendly.

Coffee was brought in and Freeborn excused himself, saying they might like to talk alone.

Fleming, in a brown tweed jacket with a maroon ascot at his neck, sat across the wooden table from Jake and Ilse and said, "It's so nice to meet the two of you. Colonel Freeborn has filled me in and he speaks highly of you. I've known the colonel for some time, going back to the war when I was personal assistant to the Director of Naval Intelligence."

"Great to meet you too," Jake said. "What do you think may have happened to Churchill? Do you have any theories on that?"

"It's difficult to say. It's well known that the communists want to take over West Berlin. Perhaps the East Berlin mayor, Walter Ulbricht, has snatched Sir Winston to use as a bargaining chip: 'Give us West

Berlin and we'll return your prime minister.' "

"I've considered that too, Mr. Fleming," Ilse spoke up, surprising her father, who'd been about to speak. "It's certainly possible but it would be such a dirty trick it could give world communism a black eye, bad publicity at a time when they're trying to win over unaligned countries like Italy and Greece."

Jake winked at his daughter and said, "Spain too."

"You're a perspicacious young woman," Fleming said, nodding respectfully.

"Your thought has merit. It's difficult to read Moscow these days. Malenkov hasn't been in the saddle all that long since Joe Stalin's death. We don't know how strong a hold he has on the Politburo."

Fleming picked up his coffee cup, put it back down, and said, "I understand you've coauthored a book that analyzes Allied decisions during the war, Weaver. I'd like to read it."

"I'd like to read yours as well," Jake said. "Tell us about it."

"First of all, I'm aware of your two incursions into Nazi Germany and your apprehension of the V-2 rocket developer, Wernher von Braun."

"Apprehension? You make it sound like I kidnapped him."

"Use whatever word you like, but you found the man in hiding from the SS and got him into Allied custody. A marvelous achievement. You are among three persons who inspired my novel."

"Me?"

"Certainly. You and two British agents, one who operated in Yugoslavia and the other in Berlin, were models for the character I created. Their exploits were equally stunning."

Jake was taken aback. "I'm flattered," he managed.

"And I believe you'll be successful again, Weaver. But enough of that for now." Fleming gazed into Jake's eyes and then Ilse's. "I know that each of you is familiar with Berlin, but the city is much changed since you were there."

He went on to describe Checkpoint Charlie, the Oberbaum Bridge, other east-west checkpoints, and the harsh strictness of the East German police, the *Stasi*. Jake and Ilse got out their notebooks.

Jake asked if he knew about the West Berlin neurologist Freeborn had mentioned. "No, but I'm sure the colonel can help you there." Fleming then gave the names of two contacts he had in Berlin who might be able to help. They'd been fellow naval intel agents, a man and a woman. Jake and Ilse wrote down the names.

"Many thanks," Jake said. He sipped some coffee and added, "But tell us more about your book. It's hard to believe I inspired you."

"It's called *Casino Royale*. I made my protagonist quite the dashing character, full of derring-do, even bolder than you. I've given him the code name of Double-Oh-Seven."

"Double-Oh-Seven?" Ilse asked.

"Right. The double zeroes indicate he has license to

kill."

"License to kill?" Ilse uttered. "Jeepers, we don't plan to kill anyone, do we, *Vati*?"

"You never can tell," Ian Fleming said.

SEVEN

That afternoon Jake and Ilse settled into their room at the Dorchester. The bellboy pointed out the two single beds, en suite bathroom, and that their window looked out on Hyde Park just to the west. Jake thanked him, handed him a dollar and said, "Sorry, but I don't have any British pounds."

"That's all right, sir, it's not hard to exchange these."

Jake and Ilse spent some time going over the notes they'd taken from Ian Fleming and the names of the two Berlin contacts he'd provided.

My daughter is quite a girl, Jake thought. Make that woman, he corrected himself. From wartime Berlin orphan to UCLA graduate to professional reporter.

He was proud of her and grateful that she'd insisted on coming with him and helping. His life had changed, and for the better, on that day in 1942 that he'd met the daughter he never even knew he had.

Jake recalled the horrendous time when she'd been stabbed in their home by a fugitive Nazi doctor and how well she had recovered from that trauma with the help of a good psychologist and her own strong will.

An hour later the phone rang. It was Fred Friendly, the head of CBS News.

"Hello there, Weaver. Doug Edwards did quite a sales job on me and I had to do the same with Mr. Paley. He's a real penny-pincher and at first he flat refused to let you go. I argued like mad and finally convinced him this could be a big story for us and at last he gave in. After all, it's Winston Churchill, the British hero."

"Great, Fred. Now you've gotta keep the lid on this. The Brits will crucify me if it gets out prematurely that Churchill's missing."

"We will. Edwards and I are on the same page with that. We haven't told Ed Murrow, Walt Cronkite, Eric Sevareid or anybody. We'll wire some funds to your hotel today. Paley said this damn well better not be a huge waste of the network's money."

Jake winced. If we don't figure out the Churchill thing I'll be out on my ass, he thought.

Friendly concluded, "So don't waste 'em, tiger, and good luck."

"We'll do our best," Jake replied.

After hanging up, he said, "Well, my little rogue reporter, we've got our work cut out for us."

A money order arrived that afternoon and Jake took it to Barclays Bank where he exchanged most of it for

Deutschmarks, the West German currency, and also a few British pounds. He gave some of the German marks to Ilse.

Back at the hotel, he called British Overseas Airways and asked about flying to West Berlin. "Sir, we only fly to Frankfurt," he was told. "You will need to take Lufthansa from there."

"Can you arrange that for me?"

"No sir, you'll have to do that yourself in Frankfurt." Disappointed, Jake booked a morning BOAC flight to Frankfurt.

Colonel Freeborn came over to have dinner with them that evening and the three of them took a table in the hotel dining room. They gave the waiter their drink orders: a martini for Freeborn, French Grenache wine for Ilse, and a Carling beer for Jake. When these arrived, they clinked glasses and Freeborn said, "I wish you both the very best of luck."

"Thanks. We'll need it," Jake replied.

Keeping his voice low, Freeborn gave the name of the Berlin neurology specialist Winston Churchill may have wanted to consult: Dr. Ernst Diels. Jake wrote that down in his notebook. "I do not have his contact information but he is likely in the West Berlin phone book." Then Freeborn said, "Your old friend Gretchen Siedler still lives in her flat on Marburgstrasse."

Gretchen Siedler? Jake swallowed hard. This lusty war widow, then a spy for the British, had lured him to her bed back in 1942. "She works for Konrad Adenauer's Christian Democrats. Perhaps she could help you." Freeborn caught the queer look on Jake's face. Was it uncertainty? Guilt? He wisely said nothing about it.

"Oh, I remember Gretchen," Ilse spoke up. "Nice lady." She had met Gretchen in 1942 and again later in Los Angeles.

Gretchen hadn't been Jake's only sexual adventure after his ill-fated and short-lived first marriage in Texas. He'd sowed a lot of oats before meeting Valerie. Some of his flings were trivial, but he deeply regretted walking away from two women in particular. Good women. They had been special and he'd simply *squandered* them. Robin, Connie. Either of them would have made a good wife. He knew he'd hurt them and was sorry he had. But then came Valerie. He couldn't possibly have done better.

Jake steered the conversation elsewhere. He told the colonel about their flight to Frankfurt and that he'd have to book a Lufthansa flight to West Berlin from there.

"Not to worry, I will see to that," Freeborn said. "You will find tickets for your passage to Berlin awaiting you in Frankfurt."

Oh, this man's connections. "Thanks. You're the greatest," Jake said.

"Not a bit of it."

The waiter reappeared and they ordered their meals: top-round roast beef for the colonel, veal for

Ilse, and a porterhouse steak for Jake.

"Does MI6 have an agent in Berlin?" Jake asked when the waiter was gone.

"Yes, one, but you mustn't contact him. That could come back and do me harm. I won't even divulge his name."

"Understood," Jake said.

"Can we contact the West Berlin police?" Ilse asked.

"Of course, my dear, but you mustn't say you're in any way connected with her majesty's government. You're just Yank newspeople."

"Got it," Ilse said.

The meals arrived and they dug in. "Mm, this veal is good," Ilse said.

Jake took a swill of his beer and asked, "Who traveled to Germany with Churchill?"

"One man, I am told, a bodyguard. He wasn't MI6, but rather an agent of the prime minister's cabinet, Seaton by name. Sir Winston was met in Frankfurt by our ambassador to West Germany, Sir Frederick Millar, who escorted him to Bonn, the capital. Millar didn't accompany him to Berlin, only the bodyguard. Winston's going to Berlin, don't you know, was not on his official itinerary."

"To keep his visit to the neurologist a secret," Jake said, "if your hunch on that is correct."

"Possibly so. Winston hated to admit he was ailing."

Freeborn put down his martini glass and asked the time of their morning flight. The answer was 9 a.m. "Right then. I will drive you out to London Airport myself. It's quite a large new aerodrome west of the city, built after the war. I will fetch you at half seven. You have your passports of course?"

"Couldn't have gotten here without them," Jake said.

DAY ONE

In the morning, as promised, the colonel drove them in a black Morris sedan past some small farms, white cottages, and a rail line. Ilse nervously felt he was driving on the wrong side of the road.

They finally reached the sprawling new airfield in the Heathrow area. In front of the terminal, as she and Jake got out, Ilse hugged Freeborn, surprising him, and said, "Thanks for everything, sir. You've been *wunderbar.*"

"You're a splendid young woman," he answered. "I know you will do well." He shook Jake's hand and said, "I'm glad that I brought you into this. Anthony Eden wouldn't be pleased but I am. God bless you both."

Jake and Ilse entered, studied a large information board, found the correct gate, and showed their tickets and passports.

The flight was announced fifteen minutes later and they followed a queue of passengers across a concrete apron to a BOAC Argonaut, which actually was an American-built DC-4. They boarded, found their seats and stowed their bags in the overhead bin.

After they accepted cups of coffee from a rosy-cheeked stewardess, Jake said, "Well, here we go, *Liebchen*." From the seatback in front of him, he pulled out up a pamphlet describing the plane. He read that it was outfitted with British Rolls-Royce Merlin engines instead of the original Pratt & Whitney Wasps.

The Argonaut took off and began to climb through a bleak overcast. The sky cleared a bit as they gained altitude and before long they could look out and see the English Channel through scattered clouds, and later the Dutch coast.

"The last time I did this," Jake said, "I was freezing aboard a British bomber and German ack-ack was bursting all around us." With an internal grin, Ilse didn't mention that she'd heard this story several times before. "Thank goodness there's none of that today," her father added.

Stewardesses brought around sandwiches and drinks. Ilse accepted a Coke and Jake a beer. He thought gloomily about Gretchen Siedler and hoped they wouldn't need her help. That they'd slept together was a brief wartime transgression that he'd never divulged to his wife or anyone else for that matter. Although he wasn't married at the time, he was engaged to Valerie and he regarded the act as disloyalty if not adultery.

"What shall we do first in Berlin?" Ilse asked.

"Try to meet with the West Berlin mayor, Walter Schreiber, and also find Uncle Dieter."

"Do you think the mayor will agree to see us, *Vati*?"

"Probably. I think he'd be okay with seeing a couple of American newspeople."

Ilse got out her notebook and made a list of people to see. Number one was the West Berlin mayor. Second: neurologist Ernst Diels. Third: Uncle Dieter. She was tempted to put down the former spy Gretchen Siedler as fourth. But, remembering the guarded look on her father's face, she didn't.

Again feeling proud of Ilse for her eagerness, Jake looked at her list and gave an affirmative nod.

Ilse then said she'd like to know more about Winston Churchill. Speaking quietly so as not to be overheard by other passengers, Jake told how as a young man he'd been a war correspondent in India and South Africa for the *Daily Mail* before the turn of the century. In World War I, as First Lord of the Admiralty, he'd launched an amphibious landing on the Gallipoli Peninsula, the objective being to capture Constantinople and knock Turkey out of the war. Turk resistance was savage and the operation failed. Disgraced, Churchill had then served in the trenches in France.

Jake drank some of his beer and went on. "Between the wars, he was elected to Parliament and warned that Nazi rearmament was a serious threat to England, but he was mostly ignored. After Britain and France gave up Czechoslovakia to the Germans at the Munich conference, he called it an unmitigated defeat, to use his exact words."

"But when the war broke out, he became prime minister, right, *Vati*?"

"Yes, and after he led them to victory, he was voted out of office. A huge surprise. Apparently people were more tired of wartime shortages and rationing than he realized, and hungered for a change."

"But they called him back to office recently," Ilse said. "He's quite a man. I hope he will be all right. His wife must be frantic."

Turbulence rocked the plane as German farms, rivers, and towns began to appear below. Jake held on tight to his beer. The bumpiness ended after a few minutes and eventually a huge airfield came into view.

As the plane began its descent, Jake caught sight of a U.S. B-47 jet bomber, two P-51 Mustangs, and an F-86 Sabre jet parked off to the left. He knew this was a joint American air base and civilian airport. "Four years ago this was the starting point of the Berlin Airlift, planes taking off right here, one every minute, to bring food and supplies to the beleaguered city."

"And saving my hometown from starvation," Ilse said.

The Argonaut's flaps lowered, wheels bumped down, and soon they were on the ground at Frankfurt.

The sun shone brightly, casting distinct shadows as they walked to the terminal, which they found to be new, spacious and quite modern. West Germany seems to be prospering, Jake thought. He and Ilse arrived at customs, had their passports stamped, and were confronted by a man in a crisp green uniform who said he had to inspect their luggage. He snatched their bags, took them to a table and rummaged through the belongings. Satisfied that he found nothing suspicious, only clothing, scarves, socks and shoes, he zipped them up, clicked his heels, and turned to the next passenger in line.

Jake owned a German Luger, which he'd collected here nine years ago, but it was back home in L.A. He doubted he'd be allowed to bring a pistol into this country.

He and Ilse walked on, searching for the Lufthansa desk. Information boards in German, French and English lined broad marble walkways. They passed a café where Ilse caught the spicy aroma of grilled sausage.

Reaching Lufthansa, they found that Colonel Freeborn had come through. Tickets to Berlin were waiting for them. A pretty blond hostess said, *"Willkommen auf Deutschland"* as she examined their passports. When Ilse answered, *"Danke schön, Fraulein,"* a surprised smile crossed the woman's face. She seemed to be thinking, "This American speaks German with a Berlin accent?" She asked the purpose of their trip and Ilse said, also in German, "Pleasure. We're going to visit relatives." It wasn't a complete lie. She hoped she could see her Great-Uncle Dieter.

EIGHT

While Jake and Ilse sat in the gate area for their hop to Berlin, an elderly man in a three-piece suit eyed them curiously. Jake noticed. The old-timer wore a monacle in one eye, was missing an arm, and clutched an elaborate cane topped by a wolf's head.

Jake tabbed him as a war veteran, a damn nosy one, and was uneasy about the guy's bald stare.

The flight was finally announced, and the man averted his gaze and hobbled to his feet.

Once aboard a Boeing Stratocruiser, Jake was relieved to see the nosy old veteran wasn't seated close to them. Ilse whispered, "I didn't like the way that one-armed man was staring at us."

"Neither did I, *Liebchen.*"

An hour later they approached divided Berlin and were saddened to look out and see rows and rows of stark, war-shattered buildings. Skeletal, windowless walls pointed eerily skyward like thin tombstones. Inside these battered walls lay bleak, naked interiors.

There was considerable activity, though. Several new buildings were rising from the devastation. "Look at all those construction cranes," Ilse said.

"This town took a hell of a beating, "Jake said, "but in five years it'll look as if it had never been bombed at all."

Leaning close to the window, Ilse said, "I'm trying to see my old school. It ought to be over there to the west in Charlottenburg but I can't make it out."

Tempelhof appeared. With its imposing beige-colored stone terminal building, this vast airport had been the world's largest and most modern in the Thirties. It was still one of the finest.

The plane touched down and began taxiing past U.S. and British bombers and cargo planes, as well as civilian airliners. Jake recalled that he and Ilse had been here one night in 1942, meeting rocket scientist Wernher von Braun as they tried to leave Nazi Germany. That hadn't gone so well. A stubborn Nazi official had blocked their departure, and they'd had to scramble and find another way.

As West Berlin was officially if not geographically part of West Germany, there was no customs to pass through—they'd done that in Frankfurt. Jake and Ilse merely entered the terminal building along with the other passengers. But uniformed policemen on each side of the broad corridor in their odd coal-bucket helmets eyed them all. Jake's stomach tightened. He tried to avoid eye contact and not look as nervous as he knew he was. Except for the absence of swastikas, the

Schupo uniforms hadn't changed much since the Nazi days.

The curious one-armed man was nowhere in sight.

After passing Lufthansa, Alitalia and KLM counters they came to an information booth. Jake felt relieved to be past the cops. He had learned German from his immigrant parents in Louisiana and had spoken it many times since, often with Ilse. Hoping his German wasn't too rusty, he asked a buxom, blue-eyed woman about hotels. "*Bitte schön,* something nice but moderately priced, preferably near the Tiergarten." This was Berlin's large, centrally located park.

"Certainly sir," she answered in English with a wry grin. "You are English?"

"No, American."

"*Ach so.* Good then. Welcome to free Berlin." She produced a pamphlet and pointed out three or four hotels in the Tiergarten area. "The Schweizerhof is nice. Thirty-five Deutschmarks per night."

"That's very reasonable," Jake said.

"Cut off from the rest of *Deutschland* as we are, sir, hotel business is rather slow. Everyone has vacancies. Shall I book that for you then?"

Jake said, "*Ja, danke.* A room with two beds for my daughter and me. The name is Weaver." She picked up a phone and efficiently took care of it for Herr Weaver. "Taxis are out in front or you could take the U-bahn to the Reichstag station. The Schweizerhof is two blocks from there."

She could even sell them U-bahn tickets, so Jake purchased one-week passes for himself and Ilse. They would have a lot of running-around to do in Berlin and the subway would cost less than taxicabs.

At the station, Ilse knew from years before how to use the pass to get through the turnstile and board the car. The ride to the Reichstag station went quickly. They found the building itself, once the home of Germany's parliament, badly damaged. Since the infamous Reichstag fire in 1933, it had been hammered during the war by Allied bombs and Soviet artillery.

Stonemasons were at work, though, patching the shell-pocked columns. "Must be a lot of work here these days for craftsmen like that," Jake observed.

The Reichstag was just inside West Berlin. A few hundred yards away, the iconic Brandenburg Gate lay in the eastern sector. A checkpoint stood in front of this landmark, manned by Allied and communist soldiers.

Beyond the gate, Jake made out the ruins of the Adlon. He'd stayed there two nights in 1942, before air raids demolished what had been one of Europe's most magnificent hotels. "The Greta Garbo film *Grand Hotel* was based on the Adlon," he told Ilse, who shook her head sadly.

They turned from the dismal sight and walked toward the Schweizerhof. An American Army Jeep chugged past. One of its two soldiers leered at Ilse and shouted, "Hey, Momma." If her father hadn't been beside her, she would have flipped him off. Instead, she just looked away.

* * *

Jake and Ilse reached the hotel, signed in at the desk, and were told that the Schweizerhof too had been bomb-damaged, but since repaired and fully refurbished.

The bellhop who showed them to their second-floor room was a young woman. As a matter of fact, Jake hadn't seen many young German men around. He knew why: the war.

Once settled in their room, he and Ilse began to unpack and put away their things. "Well, here we are in Berlin," he said, stuffing some socks in a drawer. "Does it feel strange after all these years?"

"A little."

"We're sure to see a lot of changes, but of course our first duty is to find Churchill. I'm very glad you're helping on this."

"Me too, *Vati*. It's a family affair."

Jake hugged her and kissed her cheek. "It certainly is" he said. "Okay, down to business." He picked up a phone book, flipped pages, and found that the West Berlin government was housed a couple of miles away in the Schöneberg *Rathaus*, or town hall.

When Ilse mentioned that they had ridden bikes from Tempelhof to Schöneberg eleven years ago to find Gretchen Siedler, Jake nodded but said nothing.

Instead, he called the *Rathaus* and asked in German for Mayor Schreiber's office. He identified himself to the woman who answered and said he'd like to schedule an appointment with the mayor, today if possible.

"You say you are an American television journalist?

CBS?" Jake heard a muffled sound and then a different voice, a male voice, speaking accented English: "This is Mayor Schreiber. Did I hear CBS?"

"Yes you did, sir," Jake said.

"Mister Eric Sevareid was here two or three months ago. It was a most splendid interview. Do I understand you wish to see me?"

Jake recalled the story Sevareid had produced on West Berlin's problems. "Your English is quite good, sir. Yes, my name is Jake Weaver and I'd like to do a follow-up story on how your city is managing in its isolation." He wasn't going to mention Winston Churchill. Not yet. He'd save that for when he was face to face with the man.

Schreiber said, "That would be splendid. We would be lost without American help. The Marshal Plan, the Berlin Airlift. Would 3 p.m. be convenient?"

"Yes it would, sir. Could I bring along an associate, an American newspaperwoman? She's with a California paper."

"That would be fine," Schreiber said. "Till then."

Jake hung up and said, "We're all set, *Liebchen*. We see the mayor at 3."

NINE

It was a cool, drizzly day when Jake and Ilse approached the Rathaus, a four-story sandstone building centered on a high clock tower. The sun was a faint gray ball in the dull bowl of sky.

They found the mayor's office on the third floor.

Mayor Schreiber had brown hair brushed straight back and wore gold-rimmed glasses. He gave a cordial greeting to his visitors and waved them to chairs facing a large mahogany desk, which he sat behind. Pictures of Chancellor Adenauer and some stern, bearded old German—Bismarck maybe—hung on the wall behind him. Coffee was offered and accepted.

A slender man with a pen and notebook occupied a small desk off to the side. Blond hair, black suit, looked to be in his twenties.

"This is Otto Hoffman, my personal secretary," Mayor Schreiber said. "He takes notes at all of my meetings. I trust you do not mind."

Jake didn't like the idea of having his words taken down but knew that was routine in meetings of this kind. Refusing would be rude and make it hard to establish rapport. "Not at all," he said.

"I would like to see your identification, please. A mere formality of course, but it is customary."

Ilse pulled out her Pasadena press pass and Jake his CBS News credential.

Schreiber studied them a moment, then returned them. "Both names are Weaver, I see."

"Yes," Ilse said. "I am his daughter."

"An attractive daughter, if I may say so. The photograph does not do you justice."

Ilse blushed and said, "*Danke*. We both speak German, sir, if you prefer."

Schreiber declined, saying he needed to practice his English. "All right then, introductions concluded. What can I tell you?"

Jake and Ilse spent about ten minutes asking about the economy, difficulties for commuters from the east getting to their jobs in the west and so on. They each took notes. Quietly, so did Hoffman, off to the side.

Time to change direction and cut to the chase. Jake said, "Now then, I believe you met with Prime Minister Churchill the other day."

Surprise creased the mayor's broad face. And a spark of anger? Hoffman looked up from his notes. "How do you know this?" Schreiber blurted out with a frown. "Herr Churchill insisted that his appearance here be kept quiet."

"We have a source in London," Ilse said. The mayor stared hard.

"We're not here to embarrass Britain or West Germany," Jake put in. "Believe me, we want to keep this quiet too. We just want to find the man, ensure that he's safe, and help him get home."

The mayor's cup rattled in his hand. He put it down and said, "I hope that I can believe you, but I must know more about how you learned this."

"We were tipped off by a British official who's very concerned about the prime minister," Jake said. "This person asked our help. That's all I can say."

"Unofficial detectives then?"

"That's one way to put it," Jake said. "So please, what transpired when you met?"

Schreiber looked at his knuckles a moment, then said, "We discussed our situation, what further aid Britain could provide us, the comportment of their troops here, that kind of thing. He said he would support West Germany's application to join NATO. And of course we talked politics. I am a Christian Democrat, as is Chancellor Adenauer, while he is a Conservative. He was pleased that democracy is taking root here."

"Did he mention other appointments he might have here?"

"No." Fiddling with his cup again. "Well, he did ask if it were possible to meet with my counterpart, East Berlin Mayor Ulbricht." *Damn, I don't like that*, Jake thought.

"I warned him that would be unwise and most difficult," Schreiber went on. "If it were not for his and your troops here, East Berlin would swallow us up. Russian tanks would roll right down the Kurfürstendamm. But your President Eisenhower has assured us your troops will remain here as long as they are needed. I think I persuaded Herr Churchill not to attempt meeting Ulbricht but one cannot be sure. He struck me as a most determined man."

"Did he seem in good health?" Jake asked. He could hear Hoffman's pen scratching away behind him.

"He moved slowly with a walking stick and his posture was a little stooped, but then he is elderly. I found him alert and clear-headed."

"I was told the prime minister traveled with a bodyguard," Jake said. "Was such a man with him?"

"A young man did accompany Herr Churchill, but he waited outside while we met. I suppose he could have been a bodyguard."

Jake was tempted to ask if the mayor knew the neurologist Ernst Diels but decided not to. This guy didn't need to know what else they'd be doing.

"Since you are hoping to find the man, perhaps you should contact our police," Schreiber said. This was already high on Jake's list. "They could brief you on what they are doing. I can arrange for you to meet with the chief, Johannes Stumm, if you like. His office is in this building. He is a good man."

"Yes, please," Jake said.

Schreiber pushed a button on a black voice box and said in German, "Helga, see if Herr Stumm can meet with our American visitors, today if he is available. *Danke.*" Turning back to Jake and Ilse: "How is it that you both speak German?"

Ilse jumped in before her father could answer. It would be awkward to explain that she was a native Berliner when Jake was not. "My father learned from his parents, who were German immigrants, and I learned from him," she half-lied. Perfect, Jake thought.

They spent the next few minutes talking about the morale of West Berliners. "There is great energy here," Schreiber said. "The people are enthusiastic about rebuilding our city, but at the same time defiant and anxious about the east. We have a rather split personality. We are determined not to be taken over by the communists and we know how keen they are to do so."

"Of course," Jake said. "We'll report on this."

"You will file news stories then, in addition to trying to find Herr Churchill?"

"Sure, that's what we do," Jake said. "After all, we're journalists. We'll be very supportive."

"But Churchill first," Ilse put in. Jake nodded.

The mayor's squawk box buzzed and a tinny female voice said that *Herr Stumm* could see the Americans at 5 o'clock.

The interview wrapped up shortly after that. Schreiber shook hands with both of them and said, "It has been a pleasure meeting with you. If I can be of further help while you are here, please let me know. Helga will show you to a lounge where you can wait for your appointment with Chief Stumm."

* * *

When they were alone in the lounge, a large, rather forbidding room filled with heavy dark German furniture, Ilse said, "That went fairly well, don't you think?"

Jake glanced around and lowered his voice, even though no one was nearby. "He was cordial with us but uneasy, especially when we brought up Churchill. You could see it in his eyes. I hated that the meeting was transcribed. I hope Schreiber doesn't have us tailed."

TEN

Johannes Stumm proved to be less cordial than the mayor. The police chief made no effort to speak English—maybe he couldn't—so Jake and Ilse used German during the meeting. A big, beefy man in a resplendent uniform of dark blue with gold shoulder epaulets, Stumm quickly made it clear that he didn't like "amateurs" poking around on his turf. His black hair was obviously a toupee, a rather bad one.

"I have detectives hard at work on this," Stumm said. "You could not possibly help. My men are following up every lead." When Jake asked what leads, Stumm said that was confidential.

"Do your men know who they're looking for?" Jake asked. "The British are desperate to keep this contained. I know from experience that police departments can have lots of leaks."

"You really needn't worry about that." This remark didn't answer the question and only made Jake worry more about containment.

He and Ilse tried a few more questions, but they

got nowhere. Stumm said, "I do not know what you could accomplish. With respect, *mein Herr und mein Fraulein*, I suggest you forget this and go home." He chuckled mirthlessly. "But why not enjoy a concert or visit the zoo before you leave."

This meeting was such a dead end that Jake broke it off. "Thanks for your time, *Herr Polizeichef. Auf weidersehen.*" They shook hands and that was that.

After leaving Stumm's office, Jake and Ilse were walking down a stately hall lined with photographs and paintings, when they saw a woman several yards ahead opening an office door. Dark blond hair, slightly crooked nose, beige business suit, high heels.

"Isn't that Gretchen?" Ilse said. "Our friend Gretchen Siedler?"

"No, I don't think so."

"Sure it is, *Vati.*" Ilse pulled at his sleeve. "Let's see if we can catch up to her." They'd been told that Gretchen worked for the Christian Democrats so her appearance in this building shouldn't have been a surprise.

"No, some other time," Jake said. Ilse made a face, but they walked on. "I'm sure that was Gretchen. Why do you get so apprehensive whenever her name comes up? She has been good to us. Back in the war we couldn't have left Germany without her help. I once saw you kiss her." Ilse stopped, planted her feet. Her eyes widened. "You've slept with her!" she blurted out.

A bemused grin crossed the face of an old woman

passing by.

"And you feel guilty," Ilse went on.

"Now, Ilse—"

"No, it's true. I could see it in your face. I don't see why that should bother you. You and *Steifmutter* Valerie weren't even married back then. It was a dangerous time. You were an enemy alien and she had just lost her husband. You comforted each other. Valerie would understand."

"Sometimes you're just too savvy for your own good," Jake said.

"I'm your daughter, your flesh and blood. I can figure things out. Besides, I think *Muti* knows or senses it, and doesn't mind."

"Yeah, yeah. Let's get back to our room and figure out what to do next, *Besserwisser*." It was German for "smarty-pants."

Hurried footsteps sounded on the marble floor behind them. Ilse looked back and said, "It's that secretary fellow."

Hoffman reached them and said, "Excuse me, but I should like to tell you something. I took a liking to Herr Churchill. He struck me as most genuine. He said something to the mayor which Herr Schreiber did not disclose to you. Since I hope that you find the man, I feel it is my duty as a good German to tell you."

"Go on," Jake prompted.

"Herr Churchill said he was definitely going to East

Berlin to see Mayor Ulbricht. When my mayor warned against that, Churchill demurred and said he had something to tell Ulbricht. I believe your man may be in East Berlin."

Jake thanked Hoffman and they parted. "What a nice young man," Ilse said. "I wonder if he'd like to have dinner with me."

"Ilse!"

"Just pulling your leg, *Vati*."

ELEVEN

Walking from the U-bahn station to their hotel, Jake said, "That was a good tip from that Hoffman guy. We know that Churchill went to East Berlin to see Ulbricht. Now we've got something to work on. I think Uncle Dieter can help us with that. We'll go see him next."

It was good to be back in her hometown, Ilse thought, and see all the changes. She hoped her native country could be reunited someday. She reflected on her days in the *Bund Deutscher Maidel*, and the orphanage where she had spent most of her childhood. But she was an American now and glad of it. This was quite an adventure, but California was her home, where she belonged.

Before reaching the hotel they came to a cheery little cafe and pub in the Wittenbergplatz, and Jake said he could use a beer. They entered and found a long bar with liquor bottles stacked on shelves behind it, six tables, and a pass-through window from a rear kitchen. An elderly couple sat at one of the tables, the only apparent customers. The ceiling was stamped tin, a popular material early in the century.

"Let's sit at the bar," Ilse said.

The bartender smiled and said, "*Willkommen.*" Pale, smooth-shaven face, high forehead, thinning gray hair. The man, probably in his late sixties, looked somehow familiar to Jake. "What will you have, friends?" he asked in German.

"Two beers, *bitte*, whatever you recommend." The man filled two colorful earthenware steins with Spaten Lager and placed them on the bar.

The penny dropped in Jake's mind. The man was older now, but Jake had seen his picture in a German magazine years ago. "Excuse me, but aren't you Alois Hitler Jr., Adolf Hitler's half brother?"

With an anxious look, the man hesitated for several seconds, then said quietly, "*Ja*, that is true, but I do not advertise it. I am not proud of the fact."

"You operated this place throughout the war but kept a low profile, is that right?" Jake asked.

"That also is true. It was not widely known." His lips pinched, his forehead creased. "Who are you, anyway?"

"The name is Jake Weaver and this is my daughter Ilse. We are American journalists. Don't worry, we're not going to embarrass you."

"That is good. Adolf never acknowledged my existence here throughout the Third Reich. He was not proud of our humble bourgeois beginnings in Austria. To his credit he left me alone, though he could have thrown me into a concentration camp. He just pretended I didn't exist and that was all right with me."

"I'm glad you survived all that," Jake said. "You seem to be doing okay. Say, this beer is good."

"*Danke.*"

"Maybe I could come back again and talk to you some more about your Third Reich days, but we have some things to attend to first." Jake was thinking that after the Churchill business he could get an interesting story out of this man. "May I borrow your phone book?"

Alois Hitler complied and Jake looked up his Uncle Dieter while Ilse conversed with the man. Jake found Dieter's address and phone number. He still lived in the Wilmersdorf district. "May I use your phone?"

Ilse drank some beer and gazed around the room while Jake made the call. He spoke animatedly for several minutes with his uncle. After hanging up, he told Ilse, "Dieter was sure surprised to hear we're in Berlin. He said to come out and have dinner with him and his lady friend. Things are moving along."

They paid for the beer, bade Alois Hitler goodbye, and left.

Out on the sidewalk, Ilse said, "Are you really thinking of coming back and interviewing that man?"

"Sure, with all the stuff he knows, it could make a good story."

TWELVE

Uncle Dieter's house looked the same to Jake as it had when he'd first seen it back in 1930 after the death of his Aunt Marta. Two stories, half timbered in a faux Tudor style, dormers on the upper level. Jake had been 23 at the time.

Memories swirled. He'd met lovely Winifrid, a young family friend, here at the memorial service for his aunt. He and Winifrid had taken an immediate liking to one another, which led to a three-day affair and ultimately to the birth of his daughter.

Recognizing his introspection, Ilse gazed at her father with curiosity but didn't ask what he was thinking.

As they approached the front door, Jake said, "I couldn't tell Dieter on the phone why we're here, not with those other people nearby."

Dieter answered their knock with a broad smile and greeted them with bear hugs and cheek kisses. He was husky and looked fit for a man of 72, though with some paunch above the belt. "Come in, come in, I am so happy you are here."

"Lovely home," Ilse said once they were inside. "I hope it wasn't damaged in the war."

"Fortunately it was not. Not many bombs fell here in Wilmersdorf."

A tall, attractive woman was standing several feet behind Dieter and smiling. Jake recognized her. This woman, who looked fifteen or twenty years younger than Dieter, had driven them around Berlin in 1942.

"Please meet my dear Trudi," Dieter said. More hugs and pleased-to-meet you's.

"Come along to the sitting room and we will have drinks before dinner," Trudi said. "I am sure you both have much to tell us." A maid in a black skirt and white blouse appeared and took their coats, then scurried off to fetch drinks.

Jake and Ilse settled on a plush maroon-colored sofa, Dieter and Trudi facing them on easy chairs.

"I see you have a staff," Jake said.

"Hardly a staff. Only Anna, who cooks and cleans for us."

Ilse looked at Trudi and said, "You're a lovely woman. I'm happy that Uncle Dieter has a fine wife."

"We are not married," Trudi answered. "Why get married and mingle your finances, have joint tax issues and all that bother? It is much simpler to live together, to love and be loved, without those complications."

"To each his own," Jake said. "My Valerie and I did that for a year but then took the plunge."

The maid reappeared, bringing snifters of cognac. Ilse thanked her. Dieter then asked what brought them to Berlin.

Jake told the whole story, the disappearance of Winston Churchill and Colonel Freeborn's request that they investigate.

"Of course I had read of Churchill's visit to Chancellor Adenauer in Bonn," Dieter said, "but not that he had come here. That is a surprise to me."

Jake said Churchill had wanted that kept secret. He outlined what they had done so far, meeting with Mayor Schreiber and Police Chief Stumm.

A retired cop, Dieter wasn't surprised that Stumm had been unhelpful. "Johannes and I were on patrol together years ago. He can be a pompous ass. As to Schreiber, he is not a strong man, nor as popular as his predecessor, Ernst Reuter." Jake knew Reuter had died a few months ago. "Reuter never wavered in his strong stance against the Reds. He was a great hero to West Berliners."

When Jake said they'd learned from Schreiber's secretary that Churchill was going to East Berlin to see Mayor Ulbricht, Dieter said he knew some police over there. He had served with them before the postwar partition of the city. "Not all of them are die-hard communists. Some are good fellows, happy to get a paycheck. I can make some inquiries and see what I can learn."

"That would be swell," Ilse said.

"Swell," Dieter said with a grin. "An American

idiom I had not heard in some time. You've certainly mastered American English, my dear."

Later, over dinner, they continued to fill him in. Anna had served pork roast, potatoes, various greens, and a bottle of Rhine wine.

"You must stay here with us," Dieter said. "We have plenty of room."

"Better wait and see," Jake replied. "We need to move fast on this and it would take awhile to check out and move our things here."

"Nonsense," Trudi said. "We can do that tonight in our car. It will not take long."

"I remember that Volkswagen you had during the war," Jake said.

"That little bug is long gone. We have an Audi sedan now."

And so it was settled. After dinner Jake and Ilse moved their things from the hotel. Jake was given a guest room on the ground floor and Ilse a small but cozy upstairs room with a sharply sloped ceiling and a dormer window.

"Tell me about you two," Jake urged Dieter and Trudi after Ilse had gone to her upstairs room.

Dieter said he'd met Trudi in 1941, eleven years after his wife Marta had passed away. Trudi's husband, a sergeant, had been killed when the Wehrmacht swept across France the year before. He and the younger woman hit it off right away. They had brought comfort and companionship to one another. Months passed before they first slept together.

"He is the most decent man I ever met," Trudi said, gently touching Dieter's arm. "And a wonderful lover." Said with a coy wink.

Jake smiled and said, "I'm very happy for you both." Soon after that, they all went to bed.

It rained heavily during the night and Ilse woke in her cozy garret room, seeing jagged flashes of lightning from the dormer window. She stared at the sharply angled ceiling, and let her thoughts roam. Here she was back in Berlin, her birthplace, after eleven years.

She couldn't remember much about her mother, only that she'd been kind. Ilse was only four when Winifrid was arrested and taken away. Then had come hard years in that orphanage.

Ilse recalled the sadness she'd felt when she was told her mother had died of the flu. But that was surely a lie—she had learned that the influenza pandemic ended years before. Her *mutter* had been murdered!

When she was eight, Ilse was placed in the *Bund Deutscher Maidel*, the girls' section of the Hitler Youth. Lots of memories there, many of them unpleasant.

Okay, she was back in Berlin with her father, the man who'd rescued her and taught her the awful truth about the Nazis.

She wasn't going to just tag along with him and see what he did to find Winston Churchill. No, she would do more than that, working on her own.

The day before, in Alois Hitler's bar, a photo on the wall had caught Ilse's attention. It was a face shot of Leni Riefenstahl, the acclaimed actress, director and cinematographer, now reputedly photographing wildlife. She determined to find the woman. That could be a good place to start.

It was still raining. Ilse watched drops of water snake down the windowpane before falling to sleep under her goosedown coverlet.

THIRTEEN

DAY TWO

In the morning Anna served a breakfast of eggs, sausages and toast, after which Jake and Dieter took turns on the one phone. While Dieter had a long chat with an East Berlin cop acquaintance, Jake looked up neurologist Ernst Diels in the phone book.

He called that office when the phone was free. Speaking German, he said, "I am an American visiting in Berlin and have been having terrible headaches. It feels like my brain is exploding. My name is Weaver. Please, could I see the doctor today?"

"The doctor is most busy today," the woman said. "But as you're in great pain I think I can squeeze you in, let me see"—she paused a moment—"at 1:30. Do you need directions?"

Jake said he did and she told him how to find the office, located on Pesterstrasse. He took that down in his notebook. It was not far from the Tiergarten. He thanked her and then huddled with Dieter.

His uncle said the cop he spoke with didn't know anything about Churchill but that he had a friend posted in Ulbricht's office in the Alexanderplatz. He would talk with that guy and get back to Dieter.

"Good," Jake said. "That inside cop should know whether Churchill met Ulbricht—if he's willing to divulge that, however. That's a big if."

"I think he will. My friend says this other fellow owes him a favor or two. Now Jake, I heard you make an appointment. Who is this Dr. Diels?"

"You've never heard of him, Dieter?"

"No, I have not."

"He's a noted neurologist, supposedly one of the best. Colonel Freeborn speculates that maybe Churchill went to consult him, since he's been slowed down by a stroke he had earlier this year."

"Interesting thought. If your Colonel Freeborn is right about that, perhaps that was Churchill's main purpose in coming here, rather than to see Ulbricht."

"Don't forget, Dieter, Schreiber's secretary said Churchill *was* planning to see Ulbricht in East Berlin."

"Oh, right. Let us hope my friend can learn something about that. For now, all we can do is wait for him to call back and later drive you to that neurologist's office."

Ilse had come into the room and overheard most of their conversation. "While you two are waiting for that, I'll do some nosing around on my own. You'll need the car so I'll take the U-bahn.

"What are you going to do?" Jake asked.

"I have an idea or two, *Vati.*"

"Okay, but be careful."

That face shot of cinematographer Leni Riefenstahl at Alois Hitler's bar had seized Ilse's attention.

Riefenstahl's riveting film of the 1934 Nazi Party rallies at Nuremburg, *Triumph of the Will*, had fascinated Ilse when she'd been an impressionable child living in an orphanage. The stirring music, closeups of handsome soldiers, and the sweeping panorama of the Zeppelin field packed with mass formations of those young men was immensely moving. It wasn't until years later that Ilse recognized it for what it was: propaganda. Cinematically brilliant but still just propaganda. But what a talent behind it!

Ilse had read that since the war Riefenstahl was having a hard time, denounced as a Nazi propagandist and blackballed, at least to some extent, by the postwar German film industry. Claiming that she'd never been a Nazi, she had turned to filming animals and had spent time in Africa.

Ilse returned to Hitler's place and seated herself at the bar. "It is nice to see you again, Herr Hitler. May I have a cup of coffee?" She scanned the room while Hitler was filling a cup. Two of the tables were occupied. At one of them, two American GIs gave her a close looking-over, which Ilse did her best to ignore. At the far end of the bar sat a man who looked like a laborer, with his patched twill jacket and watch cap, a mug of beer in front of him. The picture of Leni Riefenstahl still hung on the wall.

The coffee arrived. Ilse declined sugar but spooned in a little cream. She thanked Hitler, then pointed and said, "I see you have a picture of Leni Riefenstahl up there. I suppose you admire her as do I." A woman at one of the tables looked up.

"*Ja*, she has great talent, that one. It is unfortunate that she fell under my half-brother's spell as so many did. Her career should be flourishing today, but alas, she is having difficulties."

Ilse took a sip of coffee and said, "As a journalist I would like to interview her. Do you know how I can find her?"

"*Nein*, but one of my customers does, a Berlin photographer. He is the one who gave me that picture. He took it himself."

Ilse placed a two-mark note on the bar and said, "Would you contact this man for me?"

Jake entered Ernst Diels' office. The man wore rimless eyeglasses over close-set brown eyes on an oval face. He looked a little like the actor Herbert Lom. Several diplomas and citations hung on the walls, along with an intricate drawing of the human brain. Jake noticed a book on the desk by Gerd Honaker, a radical playwright.

Holding a fountain pen in his hand—he had delicate hands—Diels motioned him to sit and said, "Herr Weaver, I understand you are having severe headaches.

How long have you had them?"

"Four or five days now."

"I see. Are you taking any medication?"

"Just some aspirin."

"I can run some tests," Diels said.

Jake couldn't see any good reason for prolonging this. "Actually I'm feeling fine," he confessed. "I'm a journalist in search of the British prime minister." Sudden anger clouded Diels' face. "He may have consulted with you in regard to a stroke he suffered."

"Herr Churchill did not!" Diels fumed. His eyes shifted in a way that told Jake he was lying. Plus, he mentioned Churchill by name, which Jake hadn't.

"I never met the man. He was not here." Diels stood, placed both hands on the desk, and leaned forward. "You have come under false pretenses. I am quite busy. You must leave . . . now!"

Jake got to his feet and said, "I'm sorry to have bothered you, doctor."

In the anteroom as he was leaving, Jake gave the receptionist his best smile and said, "I'm just wondering, when was Herr Churchill here?"

She looked at her appointment book and said, "Three days ago, sir."

Dieter had driven Jake here. As the Audi pulled away from the building, Jake said, "I think I blew it in a couple of ways but I did learn that Churchill was here. Diels flatly denied it but before he could warn off his receptionist she told me he was here three days ago."

"Good. Why do you suppose Diels said otherwise?"

"I guess maybe because Churchill insisted he keep mum on this. But it may be more than that—Diels was vehement about it. He acted a little scared."

"You say you blew it," Dieter said. "How?"

"For one thing I shouldn't have admitted right off that I was looking for Churchill. Should have tried some disarming small talk first, established a cordial tone. For another, I should have used a false name. I don't like that guy knowing my real name."

Dieter looked in the rearview mirror and said, "Oh oh, I think we're being followed. A black car pulled out just after we did and it's been on our tail ever since."

FOURTEEN

Can you lose him?" Jake asked.

"I know these streets like the back of my hand,and I can push this thing like a race-car driver."

Dieter floored it and made a series of fast turns, left and right, that had tires squealing and making Jake dizzy. "Who the hell could be following us, and why?" he uttered.

Dieter kept checking the mirror. He continued to make quick turns. For Jake, this was the fastest, blurriest tour of Berlin he'd ever had.

After four or five minutes, Dieter said, "We've lost him but to be sure I'll continue doing this a while longer before we go home. When we do get there, I'll lock this car inside the garage."

Jake put a hand on his uncle's shoulder and said, "You're one hell of a driver, Dieter. Stirling Moss would be proud."

* * *

Ilse reached the house before Jake and Dieter. She took a seat and fell into conversation with Trudi. Dieter's lover asked about Ilse's background as Anna brought them coffee.

"I was born here in Berlin," Ilse said. "When I was still quite small my mother was taken from me. I barely remember her. She was a communist, you see, and later I was told she died of influenza, but that's surely a Nazi lie. They probably murdered her in a concentration camp. I was placed in an orphanage and when I was a little older they put me in the *Bund Deutscher Maidel.*"

"Ah, the infamous BDM," Trudi said.

Ilse drank some coffee and put her cup down. "There was lots of propaganda but also some camping and sports. Some of it was fun and some was not. I became a good swimmer. Uncle Dieter contacted me several times during those days."

"Yes, so I have been told. He was looking after you."

"During the war I worked two nights a week on top of one of those big flak towers during air raids, stacking ammunition for the gunners. In 1942 Dieter introduced me to my *Vater.* I was totally surprised. I'd had no idea who my father was or that he'd sneaked into Berlin during the war. He managed to take me to the States through Sweden and England. I took the rest of my education in Los Angeles. Following in his footsteps I'm now a news reporter." *At least I hope I am. I'm here without permission from my managing editor.*

"You've had a fascinating life," Trudi said. "I met Dieter when I was his driver during the war. We became more than friends. I moved in with him in '44. He has been very good for me. Now you and your *Vater* are trying to locate the British prime minister. I surely hope that you succeed."

That's when they heard the Audi enter the garage from the rear alley. The garage door came down with an audible clank and soon Jake and Dieter came in through the kitchen.

Before they could bring one another up to date, the phone rang with the curious European double buzz. Dieter answered and spoke for several minutes. After hanging up, he said, "That was my East Berlin cop friend. He has spoken with his contact in Mayor Ulbricht's office. He had something very interesting to say."

Dieter turned and said, "Anna, please bring coffee for everyone in the sitting room and we will have a little pow-wow."

"Good," Jake said. "I want to hear what your East Berlin contact said, and"—looking at Ilse—"what you've been up to, *Liebchen*, with those one or two ideas you had."

As they had the day before, Dieter and Trudi sat in chairs facing Jake and Ilse on the sofa.

"I hope my man got it straight," Dieter began. "His contact said Churchill was there to finalize a secret meeting with the Soviet premier, Georgi Malenkov."

"Malenkov himself?" Jake uttered.

"That's what he said. Mayor Ulbricht was arranging it all to score points with Moscow. Apparently the idea was for Churchill to talk with Malenkov face to face about Soviet relations with the West in an effort to calm down the Cold War. Malenkov is said to be more peace-minded than Joe Stalin was."

"That sounds just like the kind of thing Churchill would do," Jake said. "He's never hesitated to rush into things. If he could patch up relations with Russia, it'd be his last great achievement."

Anna came in with a tray of coffee and served everyone, creating a brief interval. For a fraction of a second, Jake wondered if the young woman was trustworthy, but dismissed the thought. His prudent uncle would surely have a servant who was nothing but loyal.

When Anna was gone, Dieter continued. "Malenkov was supposed to arrive secretly the next day and Churchill would come back and meet with him, at least that's what this fellow told my man. I hope he was being truthful. I'm not sure I would trust someone in Ulbricht's office."

His uncle drank some coffee and said, "But! . . ." Jake could almost see the italics on the word. "But Malenkov didn't show up. The mayor's staff was mystified."

"If this man got his facts straight," Ilse put in, "the secret meeting never came off."

"Exactly," Dieter said. "Perhaps he got cold feet."

"Or maybe the Politburo in Moscow nixed the idea," Jake said. "We're not really sure how firmly Malenkov is in charge. And we're back to square one, with no idea where Churchill is." The others nodded in frustrated agreement.

At length, Jake broke the silence. "I think that neurologist knows something about this. Diels got real agitated when I mentioned Churchill. Who do you think could have been tailing us after we left his office?"

"You were followed?" Ilse asked, wide-eyed.

"Yeah, we were, but Dieter lost him with some great evasive driving. I never saw so much of Berlin in so short a time. How many people were in that black car, Dieter?"

"I believe I saw two men in the front seat. I've no idea who, but possibly they were East Berlin undercover men."

"Somehow," Jake said, "we'll have to figure out what to do about them." He aimed a spoon at his daughter. "But now Ilse, suppose you tell us what you've been up to today."

"*Vati*, I tracked down Leni Riefenstahl."

"Leni Riefenstahl, the cinematographer?"

"Right. She's an amazing woman. She's haunted by the rumors that she was a Nazi propagandist and she wants to bury those rumors by doing something good for the world. She has many contacts. She says she can help us."

"How could she possibly help us?" Jake said. "And even if she could, how would that bury those rumors? We want to get Churchill out of here quietly without any publicity."

"Good point, *Vati*, but at least it would give a needed boost to her self-esteem."

Dieter said, "Now as to Dr. Diels, I have a friend, a retired police officer, who knows a good surveillance man. I'll ask him to see if this fellow will stake out Diels' office tomorrow and see who comes and goes. I'll see that he gets paid for his trouble."

"Great idea," Jake said.

FIFTEEN

Toward evening, Jake heard the clatter of kitchen sounds and realized Anna was working on the night's dinner. He walked in and found the young woman—he guessed she was about 25—chopping vegetables. She had cobalt blue eyes, rosy cheeks, and short-cropped blond hair.

Surprised to see him there, Anna asked in German, "May I get you something, your honor?"

Jake grinned at the old-fashioned German greeting of someone older. He'd supposed it had died out a generation ago. "Oh no, I'm fine. Back home I often helped my wife with dinner. Sometimes when she worked late, I prepared it myself. Is there anything I can do to pitch in? Peel potatoes, maybe?"

"*Nein, danke*, I have everything under control."

"*Ja*, I see that. You have a very organized kitchen here." Jake saw a plate of sauerkraut on the counter and a pan on the stovetop. "Tell me, how long have you worked for Herr Weber?"

"I have been here since 1945 when the war ended, sir. I was 18 at the time."

"I'm glad you survived the war, Anna. It must have been hard for you."

"*Ja*, and I spent many nights in the shelter while the planes dropped their bombs. It was frightening. I was in the BDM, you see." The *Bund Deutscher Maidel* was a "girls for Hitler" organization. Membership mandatory.

"The BDM?" Jake asked. "So was my daughter Ilse."

Anna's eyes widened. "She was? How can that be?"

Jake explained that Ilse was a native Berliner and didn't come to the U.S. till 1942. "Did you perhaps meet her in the Bund?"

"I do not think so. I would have recognized her. We must have been in different units. Would it be inappropriate if I spoke with her about that?"

"Not at all. I'm sure Ilse would like that. You two would have much to talk about." Jake picked up a glass and filled it from a water tap. "If it's not too painful for you, would you mind telling me more about the war?"

"No, I do not mind. As I said, it was terrible. My parents were killed in the bombings. They were in a basement shelter but suffocated when the building above them was hit and collapsed. Twenty others also died. I was all alone when the war ended."

"I can't tell you how sorry I am to hear that," Jake said.

"The Russians were brutal when they came in after the surrender. They looted everything they could get their hands on, and they raped many of our women and girls, the swines. It was horrible." A tear dribbled onto her cheek and she wiped at it.

"One day a soldier attacked me on the street. He was laughing as he shoved me against a wall. He began to tear at my clothes." Anna's eyes reddened at the terror of that memory.

"Then Herr Weber came along. He pulled the soldier off me and took his sidearm from his holster. He kicked the brute in the ass and told him to get lost. He kept the pistol, took my arm and hastened me out of there before any more Russians came along. He was taking quite a chance. He was my hero."

"Good old Dieter. He's a damn good man."

"*Ja*, and when I told him I was an orphan and alone in the city, he asked if I would like to work for him in his home. He saved my life, your honor."

"And you've been here ever since, I guess. Do you have friends of your own, other than Dieter and Trudi?"

"I have a young man. He works for a construction company. We see each other on my days off."

"That's good." Jake was happy to hear the denouement of her story. "You seem very happy here. What's for dinner?"

"Sauerbraten, sir, marinated in wine and vinegar."

"Sounds yummy." He used the German word *Köstlich*. "I'll leave you to your chores then."

"*Danke schön* for talking with me, sir."

"It was my pleasure, Anna." Jake left, satisfied that Anna was trustworthy.

* * *

Before dinner, Jake had a glass of schnapps with Dieter in the sitting room. "It'll be interesting to see if your man staking out Diels sees anything suspicious," he said. "Say, how hard is it to get into East Berlin?"

"One must pass through one of the checkpoints. People who have jobs in the opposite zone have special passes. The same is true for those who visit relatives across the line, whether by tram or U-bahn. All of these are detained at the crossing points. Sometimes the guards are friendly about it, but often they ask harsh questions and conduct searches. For instance, it is unlawful to take a weapon across."

"Could an American journalist without a pass get through?"

"Possibly, Jake, after some close scrutiny and stern questioning. You are thinking of going there?"

"Probably so. We haven't learned much on this side."

Dieter winced.

At his office, Dr. Ernst Diels was between patients. He unlocked one of his desk drawers and picked up a gold Nazi lapel pin complete with an inlaid swastika. Until eight years ago he had worn it proudly. He fondled it for a moment, leaned back in his chair, and recalled the brain procedures he had performed on prisoners at Bergen-Belsen in 1943 and '44. Women prisoners, mostly. Sometimes he felt he'd learned more about the human brain there than he had as a student at university.

He placed the pin back in the drawer and locked it. Next, Diels picked up his phone and called his friend, playwright Gerd Honaker.

Gretchen Siedler was troubled. She was lying in bed with her fiancé, Karl, a banker in Spandau. They'd just made love and Gretchen had found it very satisfying. But snuggling in the afterglow, her thoughts drifted back to two days ago.

As she was entering her office at the Rathaus, she thought she'd caught a glimpse of Jake Weaver and his daughter. At first she wasn't sure it was them, but after a moment she was pretty convinced that it was. She had scurried back out to the hallway, but there was no sign of them, so she dismissed it from her mind and went back to work.

Now here in the middle of the night, old memories came flooding back. She'd met Jake in 1942 when she was a young war widow and an agent working for MI6. Jake had snuck into Germany on a dangerous quest, had run into trouble, and turned to her for help. There was an immediate attraction that cut both ways, at least she had thought so. They slept together. Once.

Then in 1947 she was in Los Angeles for MI6, searching for a fugitive Nazi. She met Jake again and, for her, the attraction was still there. He was now married, though, and she tried to hide her feelings, but they'd had one instance of temptation, which Jake managed to resist. Just.

In the years that followed, Gretchen thought she'd got Jake completely out of her mind, and was happy with her Karl. And yet. And yet.

Her fiancé stirred beside her and she kissed his cheek. What could Jake and Ilse possibly be doing in Berlin? she wondered. They had been walking from the direction of the municipal offices, the mayor, police chief, and so on. Gretchen decided that tomorrow she would do some nosing around over there.

SIXTEEN

DAY THREE

Jake slept well that night. He'd had a pleasant dream or two but couldn't remember them in the morning. As he got up and dressed, he thought, Well, I'm not getting anywhere but I have a feeling this will be a good day. Maybe the stakeout at Diels' office will turn up something. Stepping into the main room, he caught the smells of sausages and eggs cooking and recalled the nice chat he'd had with Anna.

Dieter appeared and said, "*Guten Morgen*. Breakfast is ready in the dining room."

"Good, I'm ready for a cup of coffee."

As they ate, Dieter said, "I'm uneasy about you going to East Berlin, Jake. You could even get arrested by one of the communist guards. Some of them are suspicious of non-Germans going to the east. What would you try to do there anyway?"

"Go to one of the newspapers and see if I can learn something, newsman to newsman. Maybe buy a reporter a beer. I might even go to the city hall at Alexanderplatz and nose around, pretend I want to interview some official about east-west relations."

Dieter grimaced. He was fearful for his nephew.

Carrying a cup of coffee, Trudi came in, joined them, and said good morning.

A moment later, a sleepy-eyed Ilse also arrived. Jake told her about his conversation with Anna and that the maid had been in the *Bund Deutscher Maidel*. "She'd like to speak with you."

"I don't think I met her in the BDM, but that'd be fine. I'd very much like to get to know her."

After breakfast they went to the sitting room where Dieter began to peruse the morning paper. Ilse had gone to the kitchen to see Anna. "Excellent," Dieter said. "Union Berlin won its *Bundesliga* game last night." Jake knew he was referring to German soccer.

The phone rang. Dieter put the paper down and got up to answer it.

"Oh no," he said. "Really? Is he going to be all right? . . . Which hospital?"

After he hung up, Jake asked, "What happened?"

"My man on stakeout was made. Some thugs pulled him from his car and gave him a beating. He is badly injured."

Jake's good feelings vanished in a heartbeat.

Winston Churchill sat on the lumpy single bed and gazed around the dreary bedroom. The only window had been bricked up. After all he'd been through in his long life, how the devil had he ended up here? He had managed to keep his umbrella but somewhere along the line he'd lost his good black homburg.

He recalled the two big men who'd thrust a pistol in his back and marched him to a waiting car. They had forced him in back and clamped a sweet-smelling cloth over his face. It must have been chloroform, because he couldn't remember anything from that moment until he found himself waking up in this room.

Churchill had tried the door, but of course it was locked. That was days ago. He hadn't had a decent night's sleep since. On a plate on the small table before him sat the remains of his meal, sausages and dark rye bread. His captors brought him wretched food twice a day. They said very little, but had agreed to give him some paper so he could write.

He'd jotted down his demoralizing experience here, and also some memories from his earlier life, including his final meeting in 1940 with French Premier Paul Reynaud at the Quai d'Orsay. The German Wehrmacht was overrunning France, and the stench of defeat hung heavy in the air. Reynaud's government was about to abandon doomed Paris and move kit and kaboodle to the town of Vichy. He felt he had done his best to buck up Reynaud's spirits. What a sorrowful day that had been.

He thought back to the final wartime meeting of the Big Three at Yalta, a Russian resort on the Black Sea. It was in January of 1945, and the main topic was occupation zones and the postwar map of Europe. President Roosevelt looked exhausted and ill. The long trip had been hard on the ailing American leader. He would die three months later. Another sorrowful day.

Churchill turned to what was going on these days at home. How was Anthony Eden faring as acting PM in his absence? Opposition Labour Party leader Herbert Morrison was being as testy as ever. He would like to give Morrison the rough side of his tongue.

The new queen seemed to be getting her sea legs quite nicely. The modest but strong young woman had mettle in her bones, and she was being well coached by Prince Philip and the Queen Mother.

Churchill had begun a letter to his wife Clementine, realizing that it likely would never reach her. "My dearest sweet Clem," he began. "I know you have always been . . ." He just couldn't go on.

Tearfully, he reached into an empty pocket. Found no cigar there. Again. My god, how he longed for a cigar. He used to smoke several a day, was addicted to them.

SEVENTEEN

Valerie Weaver had just reached home in West L.A. from her shift at Lockheed in Burbank, where she worked in rocket design. "Honey, I'm home," she called to the empty house. It was a joke she played on herself. Her honey was 5,000 miles away in Germany, if he was on schedule. Jake was to have gone to London and from there on to Berlin.

I hope he and Ilse are okay, she told herself while going to the fridge to fetch some white wine.

Glass filled, she kicked off her shoes, went to the front room, turned on the black and white Admiral TV, and sank onto the couch.

Valerie could deal with being alone. She'd had a couple of solitary years after her first husband was killed in a car crash in Illinois. Then she came to L.A. during the war, met Jake, and her life changed.

She took a drink of chardonnay. On the tube, Douglas Edwards was anchoring the CBS Evening News. He wasn't going to say anything about Winston Churchill having gone missing, at least he wasn't supposed to.

Edwards instead was talking about some vote in the Senate. The show cut to commercial. A female trio was chirping, ". . . Rinso White, Rinso bright, happy little washday song."

When the commercial ended, Edwards turned to the divorce between RAF Captain Peter Townsend and the much younger Princess Margaret. It was a scandal in England. The royal family had been against that marriage from the start.

The phone rang. Valerie got up and answered it. Their friend Kenny Nielsen, a high school history teacher, was calling from San Diego. "Yes, everything's fine here, Kenny," Valerie said, then, "No, Jake's not home. He's away on a story."

When Kenny asked what story, she said, "I can't really say where or what. It's supposed to be a big secret."

"Man, that sounds mysterious," Kenny said. "I want to hear all about it when he gets back."

"I'm sure you will. How's Claudia doing?"

His wife was doing well in her new practice, Kenny said. Claudia was a physician after earning her M.D. from the UCLA School of Medicine. Valerie closed with, "It's good to hear from you. Be well, both of you," then sat again and sipped from her glass.

Focusing now on her husband and stepdaughter, Valerie paid little attention when Douglas Edwards segued to correspondent Walter Cronkite, reporting from the White House that President Eisenhower had appointed California Governor Earl Warren to the Supreme Court.

Her thoughts swung back to Jake. She had never known a man like him. Not tall, not very handsome, but so full of life. Vibrant. Adventurous. Such an inquiring mind. Fearless reporter. Great sense of humor. And a sensitive lover.

Valerie looked around the pleasant room. They'd bought this Craftsman-style house, she and Jake, eleven years before, after he'd returned from his first incursion into Nazi Germany.

Jake put up a white picket fence around the front lawn and stepping stones leading to the porch. The picket fence was her idea, the stepping stones, his. They'd done some minor remodeling. Repainted the exterior, too, white with a forest green trim.

There had been a lot of good times in this house—and a few bad ones, like the time Ilse had been stabbed while bravely standing up to a renegade Nazi doctor who tried to kill her.

Valerie didn't mind that Jake had had a fling with a young German woman in 1930. He was free and single at the time—years before they would meet—and it had led most importantly to Ilse's birth.

As her gaze swept the room, Valerie realized happily that the good times far outnumbered the bad.

She didn't pray very often, but she found herself saying, "Dear God, please watch over Jake and Ilse and bring them home."

* * *

Sir John Sinclair, the director of MI6, called Colonel Freeborn at home. He'd been pulling weeds in his garden. As a retired officer, Freeborn usually came into the office only two days a week. Sinclair told him they needed to talk.

A less experienced operative would have been worried by this. Freeborn wasn't. He changed clothes and drove to MI6 headquarters at Vaxhaul Cross, thinking, This is a bit unusual. I suppose he wants to talk about Sir Winston.

And he did. Major General Sir John Sinclair had had a distinguished career in the army before being assigned to head up international intelligence. His L-shaped office, biggest in the building, had a large window looking out on the Thames. The obligatory picture of young Queen Elizabeth II hung on a wall.

Sinclair ordered tea and motioned Freeborn to sit in a chair facing his large mahogany desk. Getting right to the point, he said, "Harold, Agent Waterman informs me that you met the other day with that American chap Weaver who helped us with the von Braun business." It wasn't a question, but his stare basically asked, "Well?"

Freeborn hesitated a moment and then said, "Yes, that is so."

"You know damn well, Harold, that the acting prime minister has said no outside help, that we alone will conduct this investigation." Sinclair waited for a response but got none.

The tea arrived at that moment, momentarily

breaking the tension. A tray was placed on his desk and Sinclair said, "Thank you, Dorothy."

When the woman was gone and Freeborn still said nothing, Sinclair broke the silence: "Are you going to deny that Weaver is at this moment in Berlin at your bidding, investigating this affair?"

Freeborn placed a lump of sugar in his tea, stirred it, slowly took a sip, and finally said, "No, John, I won't deny that."

Sinclair made a fist and struck it on the desk. "I cannot sack you—you're retired. But I could banish you from this building, and see that your pension is reduced."

"Whatever you deem best, John. But you'd be greatly embarrassed if Weaver finds the man, while our own people do not, eh? I have the utmost confidence in Mr. Weaver."

"Confound it, man, you're always doing things like this to us. But yes, I suppose that would cause me some discomfort." He stared at Freeborn and then said, "The intel you provided when my battalion was about to reach Antwerp saved us from a large portion of trouble. We hadn't been aware of that Panzer division in the area. I will always be grateful, old man. But dash it all, how can I overlook your disregard of a directive from Mr. Eden? You're supposed to be inactive now."

"I consider that directive short-sighted," Freeborn said. "Meddling, even. MI6 has always made use of all of its assets, be they British or not, when they could be of good use."

Sinclair picked up a briar pipe, fiddled with it a moment, and then put it down. Freeborn sipped some tea.

At last, Sinclair said, "I suppose what Mr. Eden doesn't know cannot hurt him. He's not been told about Weaver and I shall try to keep it that way. Well, I hope your man can do us some good and keep his mouth shut. I will tell Waterman to keep quiet as well. Go back to your roses and daffodils, Harold."

Freeborn got to his feet and said, "Thank you, Sir John, I shall. Cheerio."

EIGHTEEN

On her coffee break, Gretchen Siedler walked down the hall to the police chief's office and asked if a red-haired American man in his mid-forties had been there the other day with a young woman, also with red hair. The chief's aide stonewalled, saying obstinately that Chief Stumm's meetings were none of her business. So Gretchen went to Mayor Schreiber's office three doors down.

She had a nodding acquaintance with the receptionist, Helga, who consulted her appointment book. "*Ja,* I remember them, a father and daughter named, ah, here it is, Weaver."

"*Danke.* Do you know what they talked to the Búrgermeister about?"

"I wouldn't know. The door was closed."

Just then the mayor's secretary, Otto Hoffman, appeared. Gretchen had spoken with him several times about some Christian Democrat issue or other. She asked him the same questions as she'd asked the receptionist.

"*Ja*, of course I remember them. Nice people."

"Do you know what they spoke to the mayor about?"

"Sorry, but I cannot tell you that."

Gretchen tried her best smile and laid a hand on his arm. "Please, Otto," she pleaded.

"Gretchen, you know better than that. It was nice to see you." Hoffman turned and entered Schreiber's office.

Gretchen left, thinking, Okay, Jake and Ilse were here, but I don't know why or where they are. She told herself to keep her eyes open in case they returned. Her high heels click-clacked in the hallway.

Why am I doing this, why am I so interested? she asked herself. Is Jake doing something for MI6 again?

Maybe she should call her old contact, Colonel Freeborn.

Sitting at the dining room table, Jake was making a list in his notebook, a list of what he knew so far.

Churchill: He'd been to the East Berlin city hall, talked with Mayor Ulbricht about meeting with Soviet Premier Malenkov. Was to return the next day for the meeting, but neither he nor Malenkov showed up. If he'd been kidnapped, it happened the day before, after his first meeting with Ulbricht.

Leni Riefenstahl: Ilse says she was going to help. How, for God's sake?

Ernst Diels: Shifty character. Denies meeting with Churchill. But he did. Stakeout of his place flopped.

How had Dieter's man blown it?

Dieter tapped him on the shoulder. Jake jumped. Hadn't realized his uncle had come in.

"I found out what hospital the stakeout man is in. Care to go with me?"

"You bet," Jake said.

Dieter parked a block away from Charité Hospital. He looked around warily and guided Jake toward a rear entrance off the back street. "Whoever caught on to the stakeout might also be watching the hospital," he explained. "I have not actually met this young man. You'll recall that he was recommended by my onetime patrol partner."

They learned at the nursing station that the man they sought, Abel Bauer, had suffered a damaged eye socket, broken nose, and broken ribs. He was in a private room on the second floor, trauma wing.

Arriving there, Jake and Dieter found a patrolman sitting in a chair just outside the room. Dieter introduced himself and Jake, and said, "We are here to see Herr Bauer. He is a friend of a friend." Dieter showed him a wallet badge and said, "I was a *Schupo* officer myself. Retired now. You are keeping watch on Bauer?"

"*Ja*, the department is investigating this beating and we are keeping an eye on him for a few days." He grinned and added, "You don't look as if you're planning to bash his skull. Go on in."

Abel Bauer was a sight. Ugly purple half moons hung below red-streaked eyes, the right one looking the worst. A huge white bandage covered his nose, and his right arm was hooked to a tube leading from a drip bottle on a bedside stand. The room smelled of antiseptic.

Dieter made introductions and said he was the one for whom the stakeout was arranged. "I am so very sorry about this. Can you talk a little?"

Bauer nodded and cleared his throat, a gravelly sound.

Even though the face had taken a beating, Jake could see that Bauer was young, probably under 30. "Please tell us what happened," he said.

"I was parked across the street to see who was coming and going. This was late afternoon, before I thought the office would close for the day." Bauer coughed and then continued. "Over the course of two hours, I saw four people leave, two men and two women. There was a small car park beside the building." Jake remembered that.

"Three of them drove off from there. The fourth was on foot. One car remained, a maroon Daimler. After dark a man came out, locked the front door, and went to that car. Medium build, rimless eyeglasses. He must have been Dr. Diels." Jake concurred—the description matched his recollection.

"None of the others I saw looked in any way suspicious to me." Bauer closed his eyes and coughed again, a deep, raspy sound, his pain obvious.

He swallowed noisily and went on. "After the man I assumed was Diels drove away, I decided to leave also. What more could I see? But before I could start the car, two large men appeared from the opposite side. I had mostly been watching the office, not the sidewalk behind me. Careless of me, should have known better. They pulled me from the car—*mein Gott*, they were strong—and you can see for yourselves what they did. I managed to give one of them a good clout on the nose, but I was no match for them. *Verdammt*, I forgot one of the basic rules: check all your surroundings. Sloppy."

"Happens to us all," Dieter said. "What did they look like?"

"They wore black coats, no hats, and were *big*. At least they don't know who I am or who sent me. Three young men on bicycles came along, and the thugs fled without questioning me or searching my wallet, which would have done them no good in any case. I carried no identification. These young men called the police."

"I hope they got a good look at the punks," Jake said. "Did the police question them?"

"They must have done, but I was not very coherent and soon the ambulance took me away."

"Let's hope they were able to give the police a better description than you were," Dieter said, "so they'd have something to go on."

At that moment a nurse in a starched white smock entered, glared at Dieter and Jake, and scolded, "You gentlemen are tiring my patient. He needs rest."

Dieter replied, "You are quite right, *Fraulein*. We

will leave now." Turning to her patient: "Thank you very much, Bauer. *Gott segne dich.*" God bless you.

As they left, Dieter said, "I feel guilty about poor Bauer, but he *was* sloppy. Apparently he didn't even lock his car doors. Rookie mistake."

"How much chance do the police have of finding those guys?" Jake asked.

"Very little, I'm afraid. They've almost nothing to work with. But we do know that Diels is involved in this somehow. He grew frantic when you mentioned Churchill, and it's no coincidence that Bauer was assaulted just outside his place."

Dieter stopped in the middle of the corridor. His eyes widened as if he'd just thought of something. "When the police investigate, if they are at all thorough, they will question Diels. That would panic him even more and he'd be likely to rush off to whoever else is in on this. There must be some way for us to see where he jumps."

NINETEEN

How kind and understanding my father was to me after I first met him, Ilse reflected on the U-bahn to the Lichtenberg district.

He was firm but gentle as he helped me to see that the Nazi dogma I'd been taught as a kid was all wrong, filled with hatred and the supposed superiority of the white Nordic race. Its denial of the church and of God. It took me a while to see that he was right.

When we reached Los Angeles, he used gentle suasion with Valerie to help her to accept me. And when I told *Vati* that I liked *Snow White and the Seven Dwarfs*, he took me to meet Walt Disney. How exciting that had been. Mr. Disney was nice to me, although he smoked too much, one cigarette after another. I decided to write a story about the man. That was when I realized I wanted to become a reporter like my father.

It was good to be back in her hometown and to see all the changes. Ilse hoped that her native country could be reunited some day. This is quite an adventure, she thought, but she was an American now and glad of it. California was her home. It was where she belonged.

Ilse had learned how to contact Leni Riefenstahl from the photographer whom Alois Hitler had steered her onto. She had called Miss Riefenstahl and talked her into an appointment at her flat. She told Riefenstahl that she had met Bela Lugosi and Joseph Cotten and was now a reporter interested in the cinema. Which was true.

She had arranged for Lugosi, then an aging drug addict but still a most interesting man, to address students at the UCLA school of drama. Ilse had been the editor of the school's *Daily Bruin* at the time.

She got off at the Lichtenberg station and found Riefenstahl's street. Hers was a three-story brick building, probably forty years old. Soon Ilse was pushing the bell at her apartment.

Riefenstahl opened the door and said, "Miss Weaver, *wilkommen*. Please come in." The cinematographer had a long, angular face and blue eyes. She wore apple-green slacks—a la Katharine Hepburn, Ilse thought—and a mannish shirt. Photos of numerous actors and actresses, including the famous Emil Jannings, covered her pink walls.

Soon they were drinking tea, and talking about movies, both German and American. Leni opened a package of Dunhill cigarettes and offered one to Ilse, who declined, saying she didn't smoke. "I hope you don't mind if I do," Leni said.

Ilse said she didn't, and Leni fired it up with a wooden match. "I studied the work of our pioneering German directors Max Reinhardt and Fritz Lang," she said. "I learned much about mood and lighting from Lang, and about camera angles from Reinhardt. Erwin Piscator was an early-days producer whom I admired. Gerd Honaker is one of his disciples."

Honaker? Ilse mused. Didn't *Vati* mention seeing a book by the playwright Honaker on Dr. Diels' desk?

Leni went on, interrupting the thought. "I have also learned from your Orson Welles and Billy Wilder. Wilder has done marvelous work in America, but he is German, you know. The Englishman Charlie Chaplin, now there is a genius." She added that she had no use for Stanislavski's method school of acting, and snuffed out her cigarette in a crystal ash tray.

Ilse said that she enjoyed films by Frank Capra and Alfred Hitchcock, then threw in, "I saw *Triumph of the Will* when I was a kid in the BDM. It was so moving, so powerful."

"Thank you. I used more than twenty cameras from all different angles and heights on that film. And multiple lenses. I had to boss around a number of male technicians who didn't like the idea of working for a mere woman. But the hell with them, it was going to be done my way or not at all. My only regret is that I couldn't have created the film for a different cause, something other than National Socialism.

"Joseph Goebbels detested me because Hitler gave me that assignment without consulting him. He also opposed my filming of the Olympic Games in 1936, but Hitler again gave me the job. Goebbels was furious. He finally got me, though. He saw that I never got another Nazi contract after '38, but that was all right with me. By that time I couldn't stand the regime.

"After the war I was imprisoned as a Nazi propagandist, first by the Americans and then the French. It was terrible. Finally, a West German court cleared me. It's horrid that so many people still shun me today over those films. I was merely trying to develop my craft and also to make a living. I never joined their stupid party. There are many who *did* join and today are doing just fine, thank you, no questions asked. Well, I am sorry. Enough of that. I don't mean to wallow in self-pity."

Gazing closer at her visitor, Leni suddenly said, "You're an attractive young woman, Ilse. Lovely hair and expressive eyes. There's a natural grace about you. Have you done any acting?"

Ilse laughed and said no.

"I am planning to do a film with the Berlin Zoologischer Garten. I could cast you in it, as perhaps an animal trainer."

Ilse put down her china cup and said, "That's very flattering, but when this is over I'll need to get back to my job in Los Angeles." *If I have one.*

"It would not take long, no more than a week," Leni said.

Ilse had to admit she was intrigued. But . . .

"Are you a virgin, Ilse?"

Blindsided by the question—where did that come

from?—Ilse said nothing for a moment. But then, "Well, my father thinks so."

She quickly shifted gears, saying, "You know, I'm really here about Winston Churchill, Britain's prime minister. He is somewhere here in Berlin." Ilse went on to explain about Churchill's disappearance and her and her father's mission here.

"Most interesting," Leni said. She put a hand to her chin for a moment. "Perhaps I can help. I have a friend with the counter-intelligence police. I can talk with him. And I have many contacts in the film industry, especially at the UFA." This was Germany's biggest movie studio. "The name has been changed but it is still the UFA to me. They know everything that goes on in Berlin. They deal with authorities in both sides of the city, obtaining permits for location shooting and so on. I can approach a fellow there, a friend, who is close to East Berlin Mayor Ulbricht."

Ilse liked the idea of those possibilities. They might turn up something. "Oh, thank you," she said. "That would be good."

As Jake and Dieter drove away from the hospital in Dieter's Audi, Jake said, "Drop me at the nearest U-bahn station. I'm going to East Berlin."

"I wish you wouldn't."

"I've got to do *something*, Dieter. The clock is ticking. What can they do? Just turn me away? What I have in mind is going to the *Deutsche Algemein Zietung* newspaper. It's not far from the Brandenburg Gate. My onetime friend Rolf Becker used to work there as I'm sure you'll remember. I'll just nose around a bit, newsman to newsman, maybe buy their police reporter a beer."

"Most risky, Jake, but you always were reckless. All right then."

Thirty minutes later, a raggedy young man sat on the platform playing a guitar, badly, at the subterranean station as Jake boarded an east-bound train. Minutes later the car rolled to a stop at the Friedrichstrasse station beneath the spot known as Checkpoint Charlie. Members of the People's Police and American GIs in white helmets boarded and began examining passengers' passes. They worked in pairs as they came down the aisle.

Reaching Jake, the East German cop said, "*Ihr pass, bitte.*" Jake pulled out his CBS press card and said, "I don't have a pass, but I'm an American newsman. I have an appointment at the *Deutsche Zietung.*" He didn't, of course.

"I am sorry but that is *verboten.* You must leave this car and take the next train west."

"Aw, come on," Hans," the Yank said. "I used to watch CBS myself back home. Don't be such a hard-ass. He's not going to blow up the Rathaus." He winked at Jake and said, "Are you, mister?"

"Not today, pardner."

"All right," the German said, this time speaking accented English," but I must inspect his person. On your feet, please."

Jake stood and underwent a thorough pat-down. He winced as he was slapped on the hips, legs, chest and back. Apparently satisfied that Jake didn't have a weapon, the German said, "All right then," and the pair continued down the aisle. Jake breathed a sigh of relief.

Soon he got off at a station on Unter den Linden and walked toward the *Zietung*. He remembered the way from years ago.

There was little traffic on the broad boulevard, just a few small, noisy Russian Yugos. Young linden trees stood in the median. Jake had heard that the street's famous namesake linden trees had been chopped down at the war's end by destitute Berliners to use as firewood. It would take a while for the replacements to grow tall and stately.

He came to Humboldt University. This unappealing Gothic pile was where he first met Wernher von Braun. He glanced at the spot on the broad brick courtyard where the Nazis had infamously burned books in 1933, one of the many shameful acts occurring during the days of the Third Reich.

As the newspaper office came into view, Jake figured that the *Zietung* was closely watched and censored by the communists these days, but what the hell. Maybe he could get lucky and learn something useful.

TWENTY

When the man answered, Gretchen Siedler said, "Colonel Freeborn, this is your faithful old servant, Tapestry." It had taken several minutes for the call to go through to London.

"Ah, Gretchen, my dear, you haven't forgotten your old code name. How nice to hear from you. How are things with the Christian Democrats?"

"Busy as ever, sir. Chancellor Adenauer is forever on the move, keeping the party busy."

"Good. You mustn't get lazy, though you were never the type to do so. Now, I suspect you're not calling to inquire about an old man's health, although I must say it is reasonably good. Is there something I can do for you?"

"Yes, Colonel, do you know if Jake Weaver and his daughter are here in Berlin? I think I may have seen them in the Rathaus here the other day."

This remark was followed by a few seconds of silence. Freeborn must be thinking how to answer that, which told Gretchen quite a bit. Otherwise he would have quickly said he had no idea.

"Yes, it is possible," he said at last. "I have asked them to quietly look into something for me, something that is most troubling."

"Something troubling that would bring them here? What could be going on in Berlin that requires Britain to send Colonial Four here?"

"Aha, you even remember the *nom de guerre* we gave Jake. The man must have made quite an impression on you."

As an intel professional, the use of code names on an unsecured line troubled Freeborn. But as he was retired and neither Gretchen nor Jake were connected to MI6 anymore, he let it go.

"In any event," he said, "Great Britain did not send them—I did. It's most hush-hush. I did, however, tell him you might be able to help if he ran into difficulties."

"He knows how to find me, so I suppose he's had no such difficulties," Gretchen said. "He knows where I live and where I work. I'm rather hurt that he hasn't at least looked me up as an old friend. Tell me, Colonel, can you divulge to me as a trusted former agent what this hush-hush business is about?"

"Best that I not, Gretchen dear. It's a most delicate situation. The fewer who know the better. If Jake should need you, though, he will tell you."

"I will find him, Colonel. He has an uncle here in Berlin as I recall."

* * *

Jake spent an interesting but fruitless couple of hours in East Berlin. He chatted with a few reporters and editors at the *Deutsche Zietung*. Most of them were interested in American journalism but could tell him nothing important, especially since he couldn't mention Churchill.

One old editor with thin white hair and a gray Vandyke said, before looking around cautiously, "Prior to 1933, our Berlin press was quite liberal, but the Nazis changed all that. We were forbidden to criticize the government in any way. It remains the same today under the present regime." He glanced around again before concluding, "How I envy the press freedom you in the West still have."

This hadn't helped Jake but he felt empathy for the old man.

Later, a young reporter pulled him off to the side. He whispered that they'd been forbidden to report that it was Mayor Ulbricht who'd called on Soviet troops as well as the East Berlin police to brutally crush the recent workers' uprising. "It's rumored that he is thinking of building a high wall along the whole boundary to keep people from defecting to the west. Please say nothing about that," the reporter added nervously.

A wall? That would be appalling.

After leaving the newspaper, Jake decided to go to Berlin's television station, the *Deutscher Fernseh Rundfunk*. It wasn't far.

Along the way, he stopped at a sidewalk stand for

a sausage and beer. It was early afternoon and he was hungry. As he ate, an East Berlin policeman stopped and looked him over. A quiver began to crawl Jake's spine. He tried to look casual and unconcerned. But the cop moved on. *Whew.*

At the *Rundfunk*, the producers wanted to hear all about CBS and what kind of work Jake did for them. They eagerly showed off their cameras and editing equipment. But they couldn't or wouldn't say much about the goings-on in the communist government, or what an unnamed western visitor could have been doing there.

Disappointed but feeling that he'd done his best, Jake left and boarded the U-bahn to return to West Berlin. He'd be glad to leave this zone.

At the checkpoint he was arrested.

TWENTY-ONE

Late afternoon shadows were falling on Dieter's house when Ilse arrived after visiting Leni Riefenstahl. Anna opened the door for her, and soon she was joined by Dieter and Trudi in the sitting room.

Seeing no sign of Jake, Ilse asked, "Is my father here?" Noticing an uneasy look on Dieter's face.

"No, but we expect him soon. I don't think it likely that he ran into any trouble."

"Trouble? What was he doing?"

"He was going to East Berlin. I warned him not to, but he was insistent."

"To East Berlin? By himself?" Ilse knew how stubborn her *Vati* could be.

"*Ja*, he just had to have his way on that. He will be all right, though. He is a clever fellow. He will show up here anytime now."

Ilse caught a false tone in her great-uncle's words. His eyebrows lifted, and there was a slight tightening of his brow. Out of the corner of her eye, she saw Trudi crossing herself.

* * *

Jake knew that Russian troops were stationed in East Berlin just as Americans were in the West, and that they joined with East Berlin police, the *Stasi*, in manning the checkpoints.

This time when his rail car stopped for inspection at the crossing, it was one of the Russians who approached, a tall, stern-looking youngster with a hammer and sickle emblem on his peaked cap. An American sergeant accompanied him.

When Jake had no pass to show, only his press card, the Russian demanded, "Vat you doing in east zone? Vat iss dis CBS?"

"Take it easy, Yuri," the American said. "It's a TV network."

"So what? He not haff pass. Not belong here. Stand you up!"

Jake obeyed and got an even more thorough pat-down than he'd had earlier. The slaps at his body anything but gentle.

Again, no weapon was found, but the man looked closely through all the items in Jake's wallet. He stared awhile at a snapshot of Valerie. Finally, he returned the wallet. Jake thought he was in the clear. He began to sit, but the Russian grabbed his arm and kept him upright. "With me you come. No pass, you come. Now!"

"Come on, that's not necessary," the Yank sergeant said.

"I haff mine orders. I take him."

"You're making a big mistake, Yuri. I'll have to

report this."

"Report all you like." Turning back to Jake: "*Amerikanskiy*, you come!"

"I'm sorry about this, friend," the sergeant said with a shrug. "I'll see that our people hear about this. There'll be a protest."

Jake felt the eyes of the passengers on him as he was duck-walked down the aisle.

Twenty minutes later he was being questioned in a police station by a Soviet lieutenant who spoke fairly good English. He looked to be about 30 and had blond hair and high Slavic cheekbones. Jake answered all his questions, saying where he'd been and what he'd done.

"And why were you spying at a newspaper and a television station?"

"*Spying*? I wasn't spying, just paying a friendly call on some fellow journalists. Go and ask at those places. They'll confirm what I'm saying."

"Perhaps you were trying to incite journalists to emigrate west. I must consult my superiors. Meanwhile, you will be our guest."

With that, a guard was summoned and Jake was led down a narrow hallway and shoved into a dank cell. The sharp sound of the lock closing on the stout wooden door was like a blow to the gut.

Seated at her desk at party headquarters, Gretchen Siedler thought back to the night when she'd met Jake's

Uncle Dieter. That was in 1942. The charming, middle-aged man had driven Jake and her to Joseph Goebbels' house in Lanke to call on the Nazi propagandist's wife. They'd been in search of a letter supposedly written to Hitler by President von Hindenburg before the old man's death. That had been a reckless and fruitless exploit.

This was the day after she and Jake had slept together. What an explosive release of tensions that had been. Jake's gentle touch. The warmth of his lips. It remained one of Gretchen's fondest memories.

What was his Uncle Dieter's surname? She tried to remember. If Jake and Ilse were in Berlin—and she'd seen them, hadn't she?—Dieter would surely know about it. Eleven years had passed. Was the man even still alive?

Dieter what? She asked herself. Dieter what? The name started with a W, the same as Jake's, didn't it?

Wilhelm? No. Wahl? No. Westphal? No. "*Weber!*" Gretchen finally blurted out. Brigitta, the woman at the next desk, looked up with a start.

"That's it, Dieter Weber. Brigitta, hand me that phone book, would you?"

Jake sat on a wooden bench covered with a cold, lumpy mattress, his head cupped in his hands. He thought bleakly about the time he'd been jailed in Zurich, the result of a dirty trick played on him by a crooked Swiss banker. That cell had been cleaner and smelled better than this one.

There were no iron bars. The cell door was solid wood—it looked like oak—with a small Judas window near the top. The opposite wall of rough concrete held a small window, far above his reach. There was an open toilet and a stained sink with a single water tap.

Was there any possible way to escape this damned place? Jake got up and inspected the entire cell. The concrete walls were probably thick and reinforced with rebar. The window was too high to reach without a stool or a ladder, and no such thing was here. That left only the door. He went over every inch of it. It fit snugly into its frame with just a miniscule gap at the bottom.

He knew the door's hinges were on the opposite side, out in the hallway. There was no way he could pry them off, even if he had something to pry with. Which he didn't.

Jake gave the door a hard slap and went back to the bench and sat. There was just no way to get out of this cell, he told himself. Even if he could, he'd surely be seen and caught again before he could flee the building.

Some initials and dates had been scratched on the wall by previous inmates of this cell. He saw the name Arne Bengtsson. Apparently a Swede had once been held here.

Jake reflected on the differences between the Nazi Germany he'd experienced during the war and the communist East Germany of today. The political doctrines were polar opposites and yet there were similarities. Both were oppressive dictatorships, keeping the populace under their thumbs. Secret police. Suspicion and paranoia rampant.

His thoughts turned to Valerie, thousands of miles away, and all the times he'd given her cause to worry. She would have plenty cause to worry if she could see him now.

Time passed sluggishly. Jake got up a time or two and walked round and around to keep blood circulating and muscles loose. Did some deep knee-bends. Through the small window he could see daylight fading, twilight coming on.

He was sitting on the bench again when the Judas window opened, startling him. A middle-aged guard with a red, bulbous nose and an army field cap on his head peered in. "Do you want something, *mein Herr*?" the man asked. "Some water or cigarettes?" He sounded German, not Russian.

"*Nein*, but thanks for asking."

"I do not dislike Americans," the guy said. "I am sorry you are detained. I have a grandfather, you see, living in Milwaukee, Wisconsin."

"That's a good town," Jake said. This fellow seemed like an okay guy, so, might as well take a shot here. "Say, was there an elderly English gentleman here recently? Not very tall, maybe walking with a cane?"

"Not that I recall. No, I do not think so. Well, I must go now. *Viel glück*," the man said, and closed the window.

TWENTY-TWO

In Los Angeles, Valerie Weaver wasn't very hungry. After her day's work at Lockheed, she'd heated up a can of soup and, along with some apple slices, made a light supper of it.

Thinking about Jake, she got out their photo album and began leafing through it. Here they were on Christmas in her old apartment, before she and Jake were married. Small, decorated tree in the background. Jake wearing that gray fedora he liked. Whatever became of that hat? She hadn't seen it in years. That picture had been taken by her neighbor lady, Clara, if she remembered right.

Now here they were at the Santa Monica Pier, Jake clowning around, pretending he was going to jump off.

A snapshot of their wedding, a simple affair at the courthouse after Jake's return from Nazi Germany in 1942. Young Ilse had just arrived from Germany. She and *Herald-Express* city editor Jack Campbell were the only witnesses. The judge himself took the picture. Jake in a charcoal gray suit and me in my best blue dress.

Now here was a shot of Ilse, taken outside the Griffith Park Observatory. Ilse looking so young and shy, nothing like the woman she'd become. When that picture was snapped she was—what?—twelve or thirteen?

Now a group shot taken at a big picnic in Griffith Park. Claudia and Kenny Nielsen, Jake, Ilse, me, and even that old actor guy, Bela Lugosi. Kenny, whose leg had been wounded in Korea, leaning on a cane. That had been a nice day.

Valerie's cheek felt wet and she dabbed at a tear that had formed. She put the album aside, sipped some of the coffee she'd brewed—it was getting cold—and decided to write to her mother back in Quincy, Illinois. She didn't write to mom often enough.

She went to the desk and got out a fountain pen and some paper. Before she could write "Dear Mom," she found herself thinking about her husband and stepdaughter, hoping they were all right. Another tear fell.

Trying to divert her mind from worry about her father, Ilse went to the kitchen, where she found Anna placing chopped vegetables and lumps of beef in a large stew pot.

"Anna, I understand that you were also in the BDM

in the old days."

"*Ja*, that is so, *Fraulein*, but I do not think that we met."

"Now none of this *Fraulein*. Call me Ilse."

"All right, Ilse. I was in the Oranienburg Barracks unit. Which were you in?"

"Farther south. Charlottenburg. Did you like the Bund?"

"Some, I suppose, but not the endless preaching about the Nazis, and the party doctrine we were supposed to memorize. So boring."

"Same with me, Anna, but I did enjoy the swimming and *fussball*. What did you think of the joint events we had with the Hitler Youth? Most of those boys were nice, but some of them thought they could do whatever they wanted with you."

"*Ja*, some of them had overactive hormones," Anna said. "The authorities didn't give a damn if we got pregnant. It would provide more subjects for Hitler's fatherland. But I never gave in."

"Neither did I," Ilse said. "I clouted one who tried to take me in the face, and when that didn't stop him I kicked him below his belt. He fell over, holding himself. The other boys laughed at him. He was humiliated and I was glad of it. In your opinion, Anna, how many of the BDM kids bought into that endless Nazi doctrine?"

"More than half the boys, I'd say. They were caught up in the idea of being brave young German warriors. The girls, less so."

"I thought that, too."

Ilse went on to tell of working on top of a flak tower during air raids, helping the gunners.

Anna said she'd served in the shelters during those raids, trying to comfort the frightened civilians and bringing them blankets and ersatz coffee.

"I wanted to go to church," she said, "but they would not allow it. They made me feel guilty that I was raised Lutheran."

While Anna stirred the pot with a large spoon, she learned that both were orphans. Ilse told of her mother being hauled off to a concentration camp.

"Why was that?"

"*Mutter* was a communist and the Nazis couldn't have *that*. She supposedly died of influenza. I was a small child and didn't know any better. But now I do. Influenza indeed! She was murdered as an enemy of the state."

"How horrible," Anna said. With tears welling up, she said her parents were killed in one of the air raids.

She went on to tell how Dieter saved her from being raped by a Russian soldier. "I owe my life to your *Grossonkel*. I was ever so grateful when he offered me this job. At first I was a terrible cook, but he and Trudi were patient with me and I believe that I have learned well."

"You certainly have, Anna. You're a marvelous cook."

Anna grinned and turned the heat down beneath the pot. "You should have seen the rubble brigades after the war," she said. "Women hauling broken stone, concrete, and bricks out of the streets so the trams could run. We formed lines and passed pails full of debris hand to hand. Things like bricks that could be reused went in one pile, the useless chunks in another. Just women did this; the men were in prisoner-of-war camps . . . or dead," she added sadly.

Anna then asked how Ilse had become an American, so she told of escaping Nazi Germany through Sweden with her father, attending school in California, and eventually attaining citizenship.

The two of them continued to share memories for several minutes more, but Ilse found it increasingly hard to concentrate. She was worried about her father. Before leaving the kitchen, she gave Anna a warm hug, which seemed to surprise but please the young woman. They were comrades-in-arms.

TWENTY-THREE

No light came through Jake's little cell window now. It was nighttime. He was tired, dejected . . . and worried. Nobody in the whole world knew where he was. He was hungry, too. The sausage he'd eaten that afternoon was a distant memory. It had been at least a couple of hours since that guy had come by and offered him water or cigarettes.

That dumb song *Doggie in the Window* kept running through Jake's mind. Patti Page, wasn't it? The silly thing was popular back home. "How much is that doggie in the window? I do hope that doggie's for sale . . ." Jake hated that the song kept playing over and over in his head. Why couldn't it be an Ella Fitzgerald number, or even Hank Williams? Maybe, though, his subconscious was trying to divert his mind from his current plight.

Every second seemed like a minute, every minute like an hour. Silence flooded the room. Jake walked around a bit more, drank some water from the tap by cupping his hands. Mostly, though, he sat on the lumpy bench, head in hands, feeling sorry for himself. Was he going to be hauled before some commie judge and charged with espionage?

He shouldn't have come to East Berlin. He'd learned that Mayor Ulbricht was hated by the people and that there was talk of building a wall to keep East Berliners from leaving. But nothing else. Not a damn thing about Winston Churchill.

Jake's thoughts drifted to his gangster pal Mickey Cohen. At the *Herald-Express*, Jake had insisted to managing editor Jack Campbell that Cohen was not a friend, just a useful contact. Sometimes it was better, safer, to be close to the bad guys than far distant. To be honest, though, he'd have to admit that Mickey Cohen *was* a friend. This runner of whores, drugs, numbers rackets, and money laundering had got Jake out of some jams, and supplied useful information on the underworld. He had repaid the gangster in various small ways.

Cohen was close to New York's Lucky Luciano. He'd had no use for Bugsy Siegel and may or may not have been involved in Bugsy's murder. That would probably never be known. What would Cohen think of him now if he could see him locked up in this commie cell?

Sometime later, Jake heard the door being unlocked. Startled, he jumped to his feet.

The door swung open and the lieutenant who'd first questioned him stood there. "The U.S. Army has raised a fuss about you," he said. "We are releasing you." He motioned with his arm and said, "Come."

Jake almost trembled with relief. He followed the lieutenant back to his desk, saying to himself, good man, that U.S. sergeant who said he would report this.

The Russian said, "Releasing you was not my idea. My superiors have no fear of the Americans, but they said to save our confrontations for bigger fry than you." As long as he was getting out of this damn place, Jake didn't mind being considered small fry.

The guy handed Jake a laminated card. "This is a border pass, good for today only. You will have no trouble at the checkpoint. It has been requested that you report to the U.S. occupation headquarters in Schöneberg. I hope you will tell them that you were treated well here."

"Oh sure," Jake said, and headed out into a chilly night.

He had no intention of talking to the American forces. After questioning him, they might blow his cover, embarrassing Freeborn with some kind of news release about rescuing an American from the clutches of the Reds. It could even endanger Churchill, wherever the hell he was.

It was a lovely evening. He began looking for a subway station.

Dinner at Dieter's house normally was served at 7 but on this night it was delayed till 8:30, in hopes that

Jake would arrive. Dieter called police friends who had contacts in East Berlin, but none of them were able to find out anything about Jake's whereabouts.

When at last he told Anna to go ahead and serve the meal, Ilse helped her bring in the dishes. The dinner was a somber one; no one had much to say. The meal was interrupted once by a phone call. It was one of Dieter's contacts. He also hadn't been able to learn anything about Jake.

After a dessert of apple strudel, the three of them went to the sitting room, where Trudi turned on the radio. She twisted the dial until she found the Berlin Philharmonic performing Mendelssohn's lively *Italian Symphony*. Ilse found this ironic because the music of Felix Mendelssohn, a Jew, had been banned in Nazi Germany. "I had not heard this before," she said. "It's quite lovely."

Trudi brought out a jigsaw puzzle and spread out the pieces on the coffee table, but no one really felt like working at it. When the symphony ended, she clicked off the radio. The three of them sipped some after-dinner Benedictine and gazed at one another's worried faces. Eventually, the grandfather clock chimed 10 p.m. in clear, rich tones.

Trudi said perhaps they should call it a night and go to bed, but no one made a move to do so.

Several minutes later, the front door burst open and in came Jake, looking weary, unshaven and yet happy to be there. "Hi, everyone. Is there any food left? I'm starving."

Ilse rushed to her father and hugged him for all she was worth.

TWENTY-FOUR

Dr. Ernst Diels and Gerd Honaker were drinking beer in the library of Diels' palatial home in Grunewald. Full bookshelves covered the wood-paneled walls.

"Who on earth was that man casing your office?" the playwright asked.

"I don't know, Gerd, but it cannot be a coincidence that he showed up just after that American, Weaver, came to my office asking about Churchill."

"No, certainly not. I hope your people who roughed up that nosy man cannot be identified."

Diels sipped from his heavy stein and said, "No, they cannot. My men had to make a hasty departure because three athletic young fellows on bicycles came along and stopped to see what was going on. That prevented my men from questioning or searching the fellow, so we don't know who he is. But we can be reasonably certain that he was sent by this Weaver or an accomplice of his."

A wall clock ticked loudly.

Honaker hadn't joined the Nazi party. He hadn't liked them, had hoped the Allies would win the war and bring them down. "Ernst, I never understood what you saw in those crude Nazis," he said. "Boorish thugs. Nor did I have much use for Hitler. But then you convinced me that Churchill was behind the death of Sikorski." The leader of the Polish government in exile, General Sikorski, was killed in a plane crash in 1943 while sheltered by the British.

Honaker went on: "So Churchill turned out to be as cold-blooded as the Fuehrer. He didn't trust the man, so he orchestrated Sikorski's death. When I wrote a column about that in the *Berliner Zeitung*, Goebbels saw that it got wide circulation. Most satisfying, that was."

Diels gazed directly at Honaker and said, "I know you also blame Churchill for other things, including the senseless bombing of Hamburg and Dresden, burning out the city centers instead of military targets."

"*Ja*, he cried such crocodile tears over our bombing of Rotterdam, said that aerial bombing of cities was criminal. But then he took up the practice himself with great relish. He dropped more bombs on us, far more, than we ever dropped on him. He has blood on his hands. Blame is too soft a word, Ernst. Thousands were burnt alive in Hamburg. Including my own father!" Face red with anger, eyes like shards of glass. "*Mein Vater!*" Honaker pounded a fist on the end table next to him. His mug jumped. "I *detest* the man."

"So what are you going to do about him?" Diels

asked.

"You will see, Ernst. *Ja*, you will see."

But in truth, Honaker wasn't exactly sure himself.

Anna brought Jake a late supper, a cheese sandwich and warmed-up stew. After he'd eaten, everyone gathered in the sitting room. "You stay too, Anna, I'm sure Dieter doesn't mind if you hear this," Ilse said.

Dieter gave Anna a compliant nod and she discreetly took a chair off to the side, folding her hands on her apron, while the other four settled around the coffee table.

"So you were stopped and taken into custody at the Friedrichstrasse checkpoint?" Dieter asked.

"Right, but this was on my way back," Jake said. "I had managed to get into East Berlin with only a body search and some tough questioning. I went to the *Zietung* newspaper and the TV station, where I learned very little, only that Ulbricht was despised for the cruel way he crushed the popular uprising this year. Nothing about Churchill.

"At the checkpoint it was a Russian soldier named Yuri who collared me. He insisted he had orders to follow. The American sergeant who was with him objected and said he would report this to his superiors. This Yuri fellow and another guy hauled me off to a police station. A Soviet lieutenant there questioned me and accused me of spying. He also thought I'd been trying to convince East Berlin newsmen to defect to the

West, which I sure as hell wasn't."

"Typical Soviet paranoia," Dieter said.

"They locked me in a smelly little cell for hours. Never brought me any food. After a long while, though, the lieutenant released me, said the U.S. occupation forces had complained. He didn't apologize, just said I was too small potatoes to worry about. He gave me a pass, reluctantly I thought, so I could get back through the checkpoint. And so here I am."

"Thank God you are," Ilse said. "But they have your name, right?"

"Oh yeah. Their search was very thorough."

"They always are," Dieter said. "How many of your nine lives do you have left?"

"Not many, I guess."

"Why don't we take this up again in the morning," Dieter said. "We all need some sleep."

"I sure do," Jake said. "Thanks a lot for the food, Anna."

DAY FOUR

Jake slept late, exhausted from the previous day's ordeal. After he got up, he dressed, shaved, combed his hair, and looked in the mirror as he brushed his teeth. He saw a tired face.

He came in for breakfast. He gasped when he saw Gretchen Siedler sitting at the table with Ilse, Dieter and Trudi. *Gretchen!*

TWENTY-FIVE

The years had been good to Gretchen. A bit of gray in her dark blond hair, the green eyes still bright. The slightly crooked nose added character to her face, not unsightliness—Jake had always thought so.

She got to her feet, gave Jake a discreet little hug, and said, "It is so good to see you, Colonial Four."

Jake said "Likewise" at the same instant as Dieter asked, "Colonial Four?"

"It's the code name Colonel Freeborn bestowed on me during the war, but I think it was mostly to amuse himself. I did MI6 a favor or two but I wasn't an actual agent. Never got a brass farthing from them. Well, this is quite a surprise. You're looking well, Tapestry."

"Now that *was* an official code name," Gretchen said with a laugh.

"This lovely young lady showed up here about an hour ago, sleepyhead," Dieter said. "I remembered her right away."

"He never forgets a pretty woman," Trudi put in

with a sly grin.

"I *told* you that was Gretchen we saw the other day," Ilse chided her father.

"Well, sit you down and have some breakfast," Dieter said. "We've been telling Gretchen what you and Ilse have been up to."

Jake took a seat and Ilse poured him some coffee.

Gretchen said that after she had seen them at the Rathaus she'd called Colonel Freeborn in London, who confirmed they were here, and that she'd looked up Dieter Weber in the phone book. "I didn't know you were in search of Winston Churchill until Ilse told me this morning. I think I can help."

Jake drank some coffee and said, "You could help? How?"

"Ernst Reuter, the late mayor—he was a great man— told me quite a bit about the inner workings of the East Berlin hierarchy. I know a lot about what's going on over there. They are much like the Nazis, secretive and suspicious. In fact, a number of ex-Nazis are in their employ."

"You're not an official agent anymore, but you still conduct yourself like one, don't you?" Jake said.

"I suppose so. One doesn't forget one's training. Or maybe it's bred in the bone."

After Jake had satisfied his appetite with sausage and eggs, Gretchen took him into the library, leaving the others behind. She grasped his shoulders, kissed him on the lips and said, "I'm still very fond of you, Jake, but do not worry, I won't try to rekindle the past." She pulled away from the embrace and said, "What's done is done. It will be all above board now."

"It's good to hear that, Gretchen. Means a lot to me."

"You're fond of me too," she said. "I can tell. But you're more fond of your wife and that's as it should be. So let's get down to business and find Winston Churchill."

"Yes, let's." That kiss had felt awfully good to Jake, though.

Leni Riefenstahl called a producer she knew in East Berlin, Axel Froelich, and arranged to meet him for coffee. Each of them had served the Nazis, though reluctantly. One had to make a living.

Later that morning, in the Café Kranzler on the Kürferstendamm, Froelich was leaning across the table and lighting her Dunhill cigarette.

Leni said, "Gallant as ever, Axel. *Danke schön.*"

"You are looking well, Leni. I hear that you've been filming animals in Africa. Quite a change for you."

"After working for that madman, I needed a change, a big change. At the moment I have a project going with the zoo. And you, Axel?"

"I've been working with a young actor, Maximilian Schell. He shows a lot of promise. I believe I can get him a part in a film."

Leni put her cup down and munched on a butter cookie. Eventually, she got around to telling him that an important Englishman had gone missing in Berlin. She didn't mention him by name.

"I probably should not ask how you know this," Froelich said.

"Probably," Leni replied with a sly look. She snuffed out her cigarette in a ceramic ash tray.

"The communists have no use for the British," Froelich said, "and they have a number of agents operating here in West Berlin. One of them is a former Nazi, some kind of a head doctor. His name is Ernst Diels."

Saying, "And I probably should not ask how you know this," Leni wrote the name down. Ernst Diels. She made a note to pass the name along to Ilse Weaver.

After Jake wiped at his mouth to remove any lipstick from that kiss, he and Gretchen returned to the dining room.

"Thank you for the fine breakfast," Gretchen said to Trudi and Dieter. "Now I must get to the office. I will be a little late. I'll make some inquiries and see what I can find out for you. What is the phone number here, Dieter?"

He told her and Gretchen wrote it down in a little notebook and tucked it into her purse.

"I will drive you," Trudi said, and the two women left, collecting their coats and saying their goodbyes.

"Well, what's next?" Dieter said when they were gone.

"I'll call Leni Riefenstahl and see if she's come up with anything," Ilse replied.

Jake said, "I'm fresh out of ideas. Believe I'll take a walk in the Tiergarten to clear my head, see if I can get my arms around this thing."

TWENTY-SIX

It was a sunny but cool morning and Jake wore his overcoat as he strolled through the big park. His wife Valerie had given him that coat and it gave him a sense of connection.

Songbirds chittered in the lime trees, and a few young *hausfraus* were out and about with their children. One of them was pushing a little girl on a swing set. The morning sun ascending over East Berlin in the distance was a bright, carroty globe.

Like almost all of Berlin, the Tiergarten had been heavily damaged during the war. Although not all of them, many of the trees were young ones. A few dips and valleys appeared in the wide grassy areas, where perhaps bomb craters hadn't been too evenly filled in. The bench Jake sat on looked like a fairly new one, nothing carved in the wood painted a forest green. Strips of sunshine and tree shade spangled the bench.

He leaned back and thought about Valerie back

home in Los Angeles. It would be nighttime there and his wife would be sleeping. Dreaming about him? That would be nice. He hoped she wasn't too worried. She hadn't wanted him to go.

He envisioned her crystal blue eyes, angular face, and silky black hair. He recalled the day they drove out to Riverside to visit the Mission Inn. Valerie had been impressed by the décor in the dignified old Spanish Revival building. They'd had a pleasant lunch there, chicken enchiladas, if he remembered right.

On the way back, they'd stopped at the Thomas Winery in Cucamonga and did some tasting. Valerie fancied the chardonnay and bought a bottle. They finished it off two nights later in a candlelight dinner at home.

What a sharp woman Valerie was. Jake knew that she was involved in the design of the X-17 solid-fuel research rocket. She never failed to impress him with her clever mind. How lucky he'd been to connect with her and have her enrich his life. He thought about the day, a few months after they'd met, when he said, "How about lunch, dinner . . . or getting married?" And she'd answered, "Sure."

Jake pushed that pleasant snatch of memory aside, telling himself, What can I do about Winston Churchill? We've just got to find him. His wife Clementine must be frantic with worry. God, I hope the man's alive.

He grew aware that two big men were approaching with long, fast strides. They wore dark coats, one gray, one brown. Jake felt his chest tighten. Could these be the men who'd beaten Abel Bauer outside Ernst Diels' office the other night?

Jake wished he had a weapon. His fists were all he had and they were pretty good. He'd won a lot of middleweight boxing matches years ago in the Navy. But he knew he'd have little chance against these palookas, who were light-heavyweights at least. But he was determined not to be easy prey.

As they marched closer, one of them broke into a smile and quickened his pace. He thinks I'll be easy, Jake thought. We'll see about that. His hands balled into fists. He would give him the old left hook, which had been his best weapon back in the day.

But the guy rushed by him without so much as a glance. "There you are, *mein Schatzi*," he called out. He picked up a little girl and swung her around, the girl giggling in delight. He put her down and pulled the kid's mother into a big embrace.

The other man grinned, pulled out a chocolate bar, and offered it to the child.

Jake's hands relaxed.

Perched on the sofa in the sitting room, Ilse was reading Dieter's copy of the news magazine *Der Spiegel*. A political column on page three caught her eye. The writer opined that Georgi Malenkov's hold on the Soviet politburo in Moscow was shaky. He wasn't nearly the strongman the late Joseph Stalin had been.

And now an up-and-comer in the Red hierarchy,

Nikita Khrushchev, was said to be giving him trouble. During the war, the article went on, Khrushchev had been a commissar, an intermediary between Stalin and his generals. He'd been present at the great Russian victory at Stalingrad and was in Stalin's favor. Khrushchev now had strong allies in the party. Perhaps one day he would unseat Malenkov as chairman.

What an insightful column, Ilse thought. Hmm, maybe Malenkov had to watch his back, couldn't afford to leave Moscow with this Khrushchev breathing down his neck, and that would be why he didn't show up here to meet Winston Churchill.

If that was the case, why didn't Churchill just leave? Because someone prevented it, of course. Could that someone be Mayor Ulbricht? Ulbricht wasn't liked by the East Berlin masses. Could he have nabbed Churchill in hopes of improving his image? Ilse didn't see that really working. If he went public about having Churchill in custody, it would bring on a firestorm of international protest. Britain would be furious. NATO, too. And how would that make him more popular with East Berliners, most of whom envied the West and wanted the communists out? Or maybe Ulbricht was simply trying to score points with Khrushchev.

It was a dilemma Ilse couldn't solve. She put the magazine aside and tossed the name Nikita Khrushchev around in her mind. And Winston Churchill, too.

Like her father, she knew precious time was slipping away from them with little accomplished. Something had to be done!

Okay, she told herself. Let's have a feminine council of war, a meeting with Leni Riefenstahl, Gretchen Siedler, and herself. She could even include Anna. Ilse found herself growing excited. Four good female minds might come up with some answers.

Yes, she would try to set up a meeting of the four women. Probably Leni Riefenstahl's apartment would be best for that.

When Jake reached the U-bahn station after leaving the Tiergarten, who should he meet standing on the platform but Josh Harter of the European *Herald Tribune.*

"As I live and breathe, it's Jake Weaver, the California newshound. What the devil brings you to Berlin, Jake?"

TWENTY-SEVEN

I might ask you the same question, Joshua," Jake said in total surprise at seeing the *Herald Tribune* man here.

"Doing a story on East-West tensions in this city," said the New York newsman. "There've been some dustups between GIs and Russians at Checkpoint Charlie; you've probably heard. And you?"

"Visiting my uncle, who lives in Wilmersdorf. Basically a little vacation."

"Just a little vacation in this world hotspot?"

"Primarily, yes." Jake fervently hoped Harter hadn't heard anything about Winston Churchill. "But you know me, always poking around. Here's a tip for you. Ulbricht is thinking about building a wall along the whole east-west boundary to keep his people from escaping to the west."

"A wall? That'd be awful. Where'd you hear that?"

"Ah ah ah, Josh. From a source. That's all I can say."

"You rat."

"Here's my train, Josh. Good to see you. Give my regards to Broadway."

Jake climbed aboard the car and gave a little wave as it pulled away.

When he got back to Dieter's house in Wilmersdorf, Jake was still uneasy about bumping into Josh Harter. There was no reason in the world for Harter to think about Winston Churchill, but getting him to ponder a possible Berlin wall would make that happenstance even more unlikely. Jake didn't mention Harter to Dieter. He told his uncle he was getting frustrated, didn't know what to do next. He felt he was letting Colonel Freeborn down. "The clock is ticking," he said.

"Cheer up," Dieter said. "If Winston Churchill is somewhere in this city we will find him. Let's go and see Chief Stumm."

"But he flat refused to tell me anything," Jake replied.

"Right, but as I told you, we were patrol partners in the old days. I can get him to tell me whatever he might know."

Dieter went to the phone and called Johannes Stumm's office to make an appointment. Jake heard him say, "I don't give a damn if he is busy. This is Dieter Weber. He will see me."

The car was back after Trudi had driven Gretchen Siedler to the Rathaus. Ilse had gone off to see Leni Riefenstahl again, so just Dieter and Jake got in the Audi and set off.

* * *

They were shown into Stumm's office thirty minutes later. Speaking German again, Stumm said, "Well, Dieter, what is so important that my former senior partner just had to see me? And who is this . . . Oh, I remember now. This man was here two days ago. The Bürgermeister asked me to see him." The chief still wore that bad hairpiece.

Jake began asking questions. Did Stumm know anything about Winston Churchill being in Berlin? Yes, Stumm knew he'd met briefly with Mayor Schreiber but nothing more.

"Do you have any idea where he is now?"

"None at all. He could be drinking schnapps in Bonn with Chancellor Adenauer for all I know, or smoking a cigar at 10 Downing Street." A severe look crossed the chief's face. He made a fist of his right hand. "Listen, you must stay out of this. I told you that before. This is a matter for the police, not for civilian amateurs."

"Come now, Johann, lighten up," Dieter countered. "Herr Weaver here has performed special work for British Intelligence, and as for me, I am certainly *not* a civilian amateur. You can use all the help you can get. We will not step on your toes."

Stumm rearranged some pencils on his desk before saying, "If the police commissioner knew I was telling you things . . . Well, *Scheiss*, do you believe Churchill is still here?"

"It's possible," Jake replied. He asked more questions and finally, "Do you know anything about a neurologist, Ernst Diels?"

"*Ja*, we investigated a beating that took place outside the man's office. Three witnesses came to the victim's aid but weren't able to provide much of a description of the assailants."

"What else do you know about Diels?" Jake asked.

"We believe he is an operative of the People's Police in East Berlin. He was a Nazi during the Hitler days. We haven't been able to pin anything on him, though. He keeps a low profile."

"We know that the prime minister went to see him," Jake said. "Mr. Churchill suffered a stroke earlier this year and Diels is supposed to be an expert on those things. Apparently Churchill was unaware of his Nazi background and was just seeking medical advice."

"If he consulted with Diels it was a big mistake," Stumm said. "Do you believe Churchill disappeared after seeing the man?"

"Yes, we do."

"We will keep a closer eye on Diels then."

"Why don't you bring him in for questioning?" Dieter asked.

"I cannot at this time. The commissioner would not allow it. We have nothing incriminating on the man."

"You can't even question him about the beating at his place?" Dieter pleaded.

"*Nein*, that would cause the man to be even more circumspect, and harder for us to pin anything on him."

Disappointed, Jake said, "I hope this thing is still contained."

"My men have said nothing. The press remains

unaware," Stumm said.

Jake hoped that was true. Now he said, "Churchill had a bodyguard with him. Do you know anything about that?"

"*Ja*, Marshal Seaton. We questioned him. The poor man is frantic. He is afraid he will lose his job or worse if this does not end well. Seaton is staying at the Hotel Kempinski."

Jake wrote that in his notebook and asked a few other questions. Who was Ernst Diels' contact in East Berlin and so forth? Stumm said he had suspicions but no hard information on that.

At length, Dieter and Jake thanked him for his time and left. Walking down the hallway, Dieter said, "Did you see that *küntsliche* rug on his head?"

On the drive back, Jake thumbed through his notebook and saw two names that didn't immediately register, August Köhler and Emma Beck. Then he remembered these were the names of contacts Ian Fleming had given him back in London. He'd forgotten that one of them was a woman. Fleming had said they might be able to help.

They'd been agents of British naval intelligence, sending information on German submarines in the Atlantic and the E-boats that patrolled the English Channel. When the war ended, they had returned to civilian life but were sometimes consulted by Fleming on his spy novel.

* * *

Back at Dieter's house, Jake called August Köhler first. He let the phone ring ten times but there was no answer. He next tried Emma Beck. A woman picked up after two rings with a husky "Hallo."

"Is this Emma Beck?" Jake asked in English.

"Who is calling?" The woman's English was good, with some north German inflection.

"My name is Jake Weaver. I'm an acquaintance of Ian Fleming."

"What color hair has Ian Fleming?" Obviously being cautious.

"Brown, with some gray. It's a little curly."

"What is Fleming's nickname?"

"His nickname? . . . I, I don't know."

"Nor do I," the woman said. "As far as I know, he has no nickname. All right then, I am Emma Beck. What can I do for you, Mr. Weaver?"

"I'm an American here in Berlin on an unofficial errand for the MI6. Ian said you might be able to help me."

"What kind of errand is this?"

"I'd rather not say on the phone, but it's very important to the UK."

"I see. The MI6. That's most interesting. Could we meet for a drink at the Hotel Eden on Uhlandstrasse at, say, 4 o'clock?"

"Yes, sure."

"I will be wearing a small hat, forest green, with a feather in it."

"Got it. I'm about 5-foot-8 and will have a brown hat. I'll see you at 4, Miss Beck."

Jake then called the Hotel Kempinski and asked for Marshal Seaton's room. After three rings, a voice that sounded fearful answered with a soft, "Yes?"

"Mr. Seaton?"

"Yes."

"This is Philip Marlowe," Jake said. This guy didn't need to know his real name. "I'm with MI6. I need to talk with you."

"I'm in trouble, aren't I?"

"Maybe. I need to ask some questions about your assignment."

"Er . . . all right. I knew this was coming."

"When was the last time you saw the prime minister? Was it at Ernst Diels' office?"

"Ernst Diels? You know about . . . Good lord, Mr. Marlowe, you fellows are good."

"Well, was it?" Jake demanded.

"No sir, not there. It was after we met with Mayor Ulbricht."

"Ulbricht? In East Berlin?"

"That's right. We were walking down the corridor at the city hall. I needed to use the loo. I should have insisted that the prime minister come in with me, but he waited outside. Dreadfully careless of me. When I came out, he was gone. I assure you, I looked everywhere, even at the newsstand, where I thought he might be buying a cigar. But he wasn't there or anyplace else I looked."

"So you let him out of your sight and he vanished right there in the Rathaus," Jake said. "Then what did you do?"

"I returned to West Berlin, called 10 Downing and told them what happened. Oh, the scolding I got, which I know I deserved."

"Okay, Seaton. Stay there. We're doing everything we can to find Mr. Churchill. I'll be in touch."

Jake hung up. *Some bodyguard!*

TWENTY-EIGHT

Ilse's planned meeting at Leni Riefenstahl's flat in Lichtenberg was carried out that afternoon. Getchen Siedler and Anna completed the foursome, seated around a table. Leni and Gretchen had mugs of beer while Ilse and Anna were drinking tea.

Gretchen and Anna hadn't met Leni, the oldest of the group, but they quickly took to one another. All three had been toughened by their very different wartime experiences. Ilse estimated that Leni was in her late 40s, Gretchen about 36 or 37.

Leni pulled a small pouch from her purse and began rolling a marijuana cigarette. Ilse was a little surprised, though she'd seen this before in college. Leni fired up the joint, took a drag, then handed it to Gretchen, who did the same.

In turn, Ilse also took a hit and felt a slight mellowing in her head. She offered it to Anna, who declined, then handed it back to the hostess. Leni again asked Ilse if she would like to be in the film she was going to produce at the zoo. "You would enjoy yourself, and I know you would do well. I would direct you thoughtfully."

"Maybe. I'll have to let you know. But now, about this situation. That's why we're here. I have new information."

"Yes, let's get down to business," Leni said. "First of all, there is this Ernst Diels person. A confidant of mine says he is working for the East Berlin authorities."

"What do you suggest?" Ilse said.

Leni tossed out some ideas, during which Gretchen said, "I know of this man. He is evil. Mayor Schreiber does not trust him." Anna remained quiet but showed great interest in all of this, nodding often. The joint was passed around again, then snuffed out in an ashtray.

Over the next several minutes, the women came up with a plan of action.

"I have a Walther P4 pistol," Leni said. "Do you others have weapons?"

Ilse and Anna shook their heads, but Gretchen said she had two Swiss army pistols they could use.

Using his cane, Winston Churchill paced round and round that bleak room. His knees were aching. He had inspected every inch of the place, the locked door, the bricked-over window, the papered walls. He had escaped from a Boer prison in South Africa in 1899 back when he was a young and agile man. He saw no means of escape here, and his youthful agility was but a distant memory.

Happily, that dreadful Korean War was over

at last. U.S. President Eisenhower had brokered a peace agreement with the Chinese and North Korean communists. Churchill had worked closely with Eisenhower during the run-up to D-Day and considered him a good man. The British had lost more than 2,000 men supporting the UN force in that terrible Korean fighting.

Craving a cigar, Churchill sat on the small bed and thought of his wife Clementine. He'd married that good and faithful woman at St. Margaret's, Westminster, forty-five years ago. She must be terribly concerned about him. He also reflected on his son Randolph, and daughters Diana, Sarah, and Mary. Sarah, the Duchess of Marlborough, had a birthday coming up soon. Could he possibly be there for that? *I pray I haven't seen the last of my kith and kin.*

Thoughts then turned to Parliament. Churchill's Tories were demanding de-nationalization of the iron and steel industry, something the Labour Party adamantly opposed. It was shaping up to be quite a fight. He needed to be there. Anthony Eden shouldn't have to carry the ball alone.

He picked up the pad of paper and was about to write something, but his train of thought made yet another detour, this time to his bodyguard, Marshal Seaton, who had failed to protect him. Where was Seaton now? What action was taken after he reported to London?

TWENTY-NINE

Repairs from bomb damage were still under way at the Hotel Eden. In the bar, Jake saw that heavy wood supports were helping to stabilize a sagging ceiling. He ran his eyes around the room and spotted a woman in a green hat with a feather at a rear booth. She was staring at him.

The place was abuzz with the chatter of men and women drinking beer and liquor at the bar and at tables. Smoke hung heavy in the air. One of the support timbers partially blocked his view of Emma Beck and would do the same to anyone who would observe them once he was seated with her.

Jake stepped up to the woman and said, "My name is Jake Weaver. May I join you?" She had a cigarette going and another was snuffed out in a glass ashtray.

"Certainly, Mr. Weaver."

Jake had to duck beneath the supporting slab of wood to sit opposite her. She faced the entrance, so he could not, which made him a little uneasy, but there was nothing to do about it.

"I am Emma Beck, of course. May I offer you a cigarette?"

"No thank you, I don't smoke."

"Then I will not subject you to my fumes," she said, and snuffed out her cigarette in the ashtray. "You must call me Emma." She had light blue eyes, rosy cheeks and full lips—looked to be about 40. All in all, a mature, handsome woman. A half-full glass of what looked like whisky sat in front of her.

"And please call me Jake."

"They have good Kentucky bourbon here," Emma said. "They barter it from your American soldiers. That is what I'm having."

A young but hard-looking waitress with weary eyes approached, and Jake said in German, "I'll have the same as the lady's, *bitte*. Ice, not much water."

When the girl was gone, Emma said, "After we spoke on the phone, I called Ian Fleming to confirm that he knew of you. One must be careful, you know."

"Of course. Can't blame you."

She lowered her voice and said, "He confided that you are in search of the British prime minister, who seems to have disappeared here."

"That's right, Emma, but before we go into that, please tell me a little about yourself."

She chuckled and said, "Curious newsman, aren't you? Ian told me you are in American television. All right then, my husband and I have a used-furniture business. There is a lot of furniture in damaged and abandoned buildings which we collect and repair.

There is quite a market for that as West Berlin recovers and people reestablish their homes. We have a son at university in Hamburg. He is 20. We lost our daughter Christina during the war."

"I'm very sorry to hear that. Must have been hard for you."

"Thank you. It was and still is." Emma's eyes scanned the room. She spoke softly again, saying, "We detested the Nazis. Christina's death only hardened our determination to help the British."

The waitress reappeared and set down Jake's glass of bourbon. After she left, he raised it and said, "*Prosit*," the traditional German toast. Emma smiled and clinked her glass against his. "Now, tell me about yourself, please."

Jake told her that he'd been a newspaperman in Los Angeles for several years and recently moved into television. He had a wife and daughter. He had done some unofficial sleuthing during the war for MI6 and Colonel Freeborn.

"Do you know of Colonel Freeborn?"

"Ian Fleming has mentioned the colonel," Emma said. "You are a most interesting man." She scrunched up her forehead in thought a moment and said, "Say, my husband told me something the other day that may or may not have some connection to this. One of our customers is a carpenter, Ekhard by name, who has almost more work than he can handle, what with all the rebuilding going on. He told Rudi, that's my husband, about a curious job of remodeling he'd done at a house near the east-west boundary."

Emma studied the room again, leaned closer, and spoke in little more than a whisper. "Ekhard converted a bedroom into something quite different. He and his crew bricked over the window, reinforced the walls, and replaced the wooden door with a steel one. He was mystified at why the owner should want such a thing done, but the money was good."

Just the kind of place where someone could be imprisoned, Jake thought as he sipped some bourbon. "Do you know where this house is?"

"Somewhere near the Oberbaum Bridge, as I recall. The owner told the carpenter not to mention the job to anyone, but he and my husband are close friends, so in confidence he told Rudi."

"And your husband always shares confidences with his good wife," Jake said. "Yeah, that's damned curious. Would you happen to know the owner's name?" He wondered if it was Ernst Diels.

"No, I don't think he told Rudi that."

"Can you find out exactly where this house is?"

"Rudi would be reluctant to divulge that to a stranger, which you would be to him, if he even knows, that is. He would not want to endanger Ekhard, who in any case might refuse to say."

"I know this is asking a lot and that it's a longshot," Jake said, "but would you try? This could be immensely important."

"I'm aware of that. All right, I will call Rudi and ask him, but I cannot guarantee anything. There is a phone in the rear." With that, Emma Beck got up and went to the phone.

She was back five minutes later. "Rudi was hesitant, but I convinced him this is important. He will ask Ekhard tonight. Where can I reach you?"

"I am staying with my uncle," Jake said, and gave her the phone number.

Emma scribbled it on a cocktail napkin and tucked it in her purse. "Do you think that Winston Churchill is being held prisoner in that room?" she asked.

"Over the years, Emma, I've found that almost anything is possible." After all, Jake had met such people as President Roosevelt and even Joseph Goebbels face to face. Had found Wernher von Braun and got him into U.S. hands. Yes, anything was possible.

THIRTY

Sitting on her sofa in her home on Saturn Avenue, Valerie Weaver reflected on her first husband Jim, who had died when his car crashed off an icy road near Macomb, Illinois in the winter of 1940. She had loved Jim, a decent guy and devoted husband.

After grieving for several months, she decided to move to Los Angeles and start a whole new life for herself. Her mother had objected, pleading with her not to move so far away, but Valerie had made up her mind. There was no stopping her.

She was a tool designer, a rare job for a woman at that time, and got hired on at North American Aviation.

She met Jake the next year. She'd never known anyone like the fun-loving, feisty risk-taker that he was. They were married in 1942 and she'd never regretted it, even though he gave her several worries, like the two times he'd gone into Nazi Germany during the war. Nazi Germany! How relieved she was when he came home alive each time. And the great surprise when he brought back a daughter she had known nothing about. She quickly took to the 12-year-old girl and happily accepted her as her stepdaughter.

Now Jake was back there again. Even though the Nazis were long gone, Berlin was still a perilous place, half of it ruled by the communists.

She got up, went to the fireplace and took down the George Cross from its place of honor on the mantel, and studied it. The royal blue ribbon and silver cross were exquisite. Jake had been awarded this medal for getting the rocket scientist von Braun into Allied hands in 1945. A most deserved honor.

She ran her fingers over the ribbon. How she wished those fingers could be caressing Jake's face at this moment, that she could be holding him in her arms.

"Oh, Lord, please watch over that crazy husband of mine," she whispered.

Gerd Honaker had a problem. It was a huge surprise when, less than two weeks ago, he got the tip that Churchill was coming to Berlin. Thanks to his clever friend on Ulbricht's staff, he had abducted the man he detested, perhaps the most famous man in the world. But what was his next step? The opportunity had come up so fast he hadn't been able to plan it all out.

Sitting in an easy chair in his home, Honaker fiddled with his fountain pen, twisting it back and forth like a baton twirler, trying to think. He often did his best thinking with that pen in hand. The vile, cocksure man was locked up, right here in this very house. But now that he had him, he couldn't just let him rot in the makeshift cell forever. He would have to eliminate him and somehow make the body disappear.

But how to do that? How to take that next and final step? He should have had that all planned by now. He'd written half a play.

You are supposed to be such a great playwright, Honaker goaded himself, write a good ending to this one. The play he was writing now, about the Pope's failure to condemn Hitler for his slaughter of the Jews, he knew how *that* one would end. Words floated across his mind like a passing parade. Scene. Act. Story arc. Stage. Theater.

Theater? Now it came to him. The Hyperion Theatre, bomb damaged, about to be razed to make way for an apartment building. He had toured the ruins with a group of drama friends a month or so ago. The roof, the auditorium and the proscenium were wrecked but still partially standing. The below-ground prop rooms where scenery and costumes were stored remained mostly intact.

The developer was going to demolish what remained standing and fill the basement with the rubble. This was scheduled to happen soon, in the next few days.

He could put his man down there and let him be buried under tons of broken concrete, steel, and masonry. The pen flashing back and forth even faster now. Feeling himself growing feverish with excitement.

Buried alive, maybe? Even better. The man being such an actor, such a hypocritical orator, that would be just the thing.

The Hyperion was in East Berlin, just a few meters inside the boundary. That shouldn't be a problem. The roped-off construction zone spanned the border. The waiting bulldozers were actually on the West Berlin side.

Once the above-ground remains were dynamited, the 'dozers would roll in and level it all off. Winston Churchill would be buried beneath Berlin rubble that he himself had caused with his relentless, immoral bombing. What could be more perfect!

Dieter's grandfather clock chimed 9 p.m. He, Jake, Ilse and Trudi were drinking coffee in the sitting room, having decided they'd had enough hard drinks lately. Jake had told them about calling the bodyguard and finding that Churchill had been snatched at the East Berlin Rathaus just after meeting with Mayor Ulbricht. "It helps to have that pinpointed." He also told of his meeting with Emma Beck, a one-time informant for British naval intelligence.

Some swing-band music was coming from the radio when the phone rang.

Dieter got up to answer and said, "Hallo . . . Yes, *Frau* Beck, Jake Weaver is here. One moment, please."

When Jake took the receiver, he said, "Good evening, Emma. Thank you for calling. What did your husband say?"

"That the master carpenter knows this is important, but that he must be careful. Ekhard would like to meet you and satisfy himself about you before giving up the address of that house."

"Okay, if that's what it'll take. I really need to know."

"I thought you would say that, Jake. Being a carpenter, he starts work early. He wants to know if you would meet him at 7 in the morning at Café Europa on Hardenbergstrasse. Do you know where that is?"

"No, but I can find it. Maybe my uncle knows. Café Europa, 7 a.m., and his name is Ekhard, right?"

"Yes, that's it."

"All right, Emma. Have your husband tell him I'll be there. Many thanks."

After hanging up, Jake said, "Damn, another hoop to jump through." But it was the best lead he'd had yet.

He would have to get up early if he was going to meet this carpenter at 7. In the guest bedroom he'd been using, an alarm clock sat on the bedside table. Jake set it for 5:30, then brushed his teeth and got into his pajamas.

He crawled into bed and said a little prayer for Valerie. Before sleep came he pondered how he would play it with this Ekhard person. He just *had* to find that house with the altered bedroom.

Jake had a weird dream that night. He was driving home after work but kept coming to streets he'd never known, had never heard of. He made turn after turn but just couldn't manage to find his own Saturn

Avenue. Where the devil was it? He was hopelessly lost in strange territory.

THIRTY-ONE

DAY FIVE

In the morning, it was easy to spot Ekhard. Only one man in Café Europa wore gray overalls and a long-billed painter's cap. A tool bag lay on a chair beside him. He stood at a table where he could watch people coming in. A coffee cup and a plate of croissants sat on the table. The place was packed with early-morning Berliners.

Jake waved, strode up to the man and said, "You're Ekhard, right? I'm Jake Weaver." Ekhard nodded and they sat down. The carpenter was burly and muscular with a weathered face. A face that bore a very guarded look.

"Good to meet you," Jake said. Before he could go further, a buxom waitress in a dirndl came up and asked what he would have. "The same as this gentleman, coffee and one of those croissants, *bitte schön.*"

Ekhard spoke first when the girl was gone: "Rudi told me who you are, but he has never met you. How am I to know you're not an East Berlin agent?"

Jake extracted his CBS press card and California driver's license from his wallet and handed them to the carpenter. He studied them and said, "If you're an American, how is it that you speak German?"

"My parents were German immigrants and I learned from them."

"That's a good story, but these documents could be forged. The *Stasi* are good at that," he said, handing them back. "How am I to know—"

"You don't," Jake interrupted, "but there's got to be some trust here."

"Why? I do not know you, nor do I know that those papers are genuine."

Jake's order arrived. He thanked the girl and drank some coffee. "Rudi must have told you I suspect you were building a prison cell," Jake said. "The people I'm helping need to know where that house is."

"I am sworn to secrecy on that."

"And you're a man who keeps his word," Jake said. He scanned the room to be sure no one was listening. He stared hard into the carpenter's face and said in a near whisper, "Tell me, and I promise no one will know."

"I cannot."

This guy was sure obstinate. It would take some tough talk to bring him around. "If I tell the authorities what you did to that room," Jake said, "your employer will be all over your ass, won't he? And I'm sure there are code violations. The cops would bring you in for questioning." Jake had no idea about that, but it sounded good.

"You are bluffing," Ekhard said. "What do you know about building codes?"

"I know plenty. I have a cousin in the city engineering department," Jake dissembled with a straight face.

"You are lying!"

Jake stared directly into the man's eyes. "Have it your way, then. I'll just go to the police."

Ekhard held the gaze for a long moment, then blinked. "I cannot give you that address."

"The police will be very interested in what I have to say."

Ekhard's face turned pale. At last, he said, "*Nein, bitte.* All right then, you give me no choice."

Ekhard remained motionless for several seconds, then finally reached into a pocket on his overalls and pulled out what looked like a receipt. He studied it a moment and then said, "The address is Number 14 Spreewegstrasse. You must tell no one."

"I won't," Jake said as he wrote the address in his notebook. "You have my word. No one will know."

"*Gut, danke.* Say, Rudi told me you are staying with your uncle."

"That's right. Dieter Weber."

"I see. Now, if you will excuse me, I must get to work." Ekhard got up, snarled, "Keep your promise," and walked off.

Jake watched him leave. He finished the croissant, drank some coffee, and threw down a few Deutschmarks on the table. *Ekhard got a free breakfast, but the stubborn fool earned it.* Jake got up and also left Café Europa.

Out on the street, though, he scolded himself. *I never should've given that guy Dieter's name. What was I thinking?*

Back at Dieter's by 8:30, Jake was told by Anna that she had *früstück* ready for him. "Thanks, but I've already had coffee and a croissant. Maybe just a few strips of bacon." He sat at the table where Ilse, Dieter, and Trudi drank coffee over the remains of their meal.

"How did it go, *Vati*?" Ilse asked.

"Pretty well. The carpenter was damned reluctant at first, but I told him if he didn't come through I'd see that he landed in trouble. He gave me the address."

"Of the house where he rebuilt that room?" Ilse said.

"Yep."

"Excellent. What's the address?"

Jake told her and she wrote it down.

"I want to go there today," Jake said. "I think they've got Churchill in that room."

"Most dangerous," Dieter said, "but it's something we have to do."

"We?"

"Of course. You'll need backup. We will both be armed."

Jake didn't know it, but minutes later Ilse went to the phone and quietly called Leni Riefenstahl.

* * *

At the house on Spreewegstrasse, Ernst Diels and Gerd Honaker sat in chairs, drinking schnapps and talking. "Have you decided?" Diels asked. "You are going to kill him or ask for ransom?"

Diels had been growing anxious. *Will this thing all go bad? Would I be arrested by the British?* Diels had been a Nazi all along, but a friendship since childhood nevertheless linked the two. He was the one who'd turned Honaker around, suggesting he had proof from the Abwehr that Churchill had arranged for the Polish leader Sikorski to die. It was a lie, but Diels didn't care—he was glad to convert his friend to the cause. After that, Honaker had railed at the RAF's obliteration of defenseless Dresden, as had all Germans, Nazi or not. Honaker even more so. It had become an obsession with him—he'd been out of control for days. A dark aching fear was consuming the man. This had gone too far, much too far.

Even with his contacts, Diels could see no way that Churchill could be quietly released at this point without Honaker being implicated. Or himself either.

"Ransom would be difficult to arrange," the playwright said. "No, executing him is best. His bombs killed my father! When I was a boy, my good V*ater* taught me how to build model boats. We would sail them on weekends at the Biddenhalster. We also went rabbit hunting in the countryside. He taught me how to handle and care for a rifle.

"Father was a strict disciplinarian, but fair and

even-handed about it. He was 55 and in good health when Hamburg was fire bombed—what should have been his golden years were stolen from him by the British. Those *Schweinhunden* could have targeted the industrial zone, but *nein*, Churchill had to go and burn out the city center. It will give me great satisfaction to send that evil man to hell."

Diels winced.

THIRTY-TWO

Before noon, Dieter found Number 14 Spreeweg-strasse and parked the Audi two doors down. He and Jake had loaded Walther pistols in their coat pockets. A light rain sprinkled down.

"How shall we do this?" Jake said.

"We'll march up to the door and ask to see the owner. I will show my police badge, which is outdated but no one will notice."

They strode to the house, an elaborate, one-story bungalow with a high, green-shingled roof and a covered portico. Jake put a hand on his pistol. It was little comfort.

Dieter pushed the bell. The door opened moments later and there stood a middle-aged man with blond hair and steely green eyes. It was the playwright Gerd Honaker, but they didn't know that.

"*Ja*?" he said coldly.

Dieter showed his wallet badge and said, "We are the police. We believe a room here was altered without a proper permit. We need to see that room."

The man frowned. "Do you have a warrant?"

"Certainly." Dieter pulled a piece of paper from a pocket and held it up without letting the man get a good look at it. It was a receipt from a garage where he'd had his car serviced. "If we find no code violations we'll be on our way," he said.

The owner stood his ground. "And if I say to hell with you and shut the door?"

"Then we will break it down and arrest you for interfering with a police investigation."

They stared at each other. Who would blink first? It was a long moment.

Finally, it was the man in the doorway. "You must let me see that warrant, if that's even what it is." Said with pinched-lips determination.

Jake and Dieter looked at each other for several seconds. Dieter knew he couldn't allow this man to see that garage receipt. He decided, Okay then, we'll pull out our guns and force our way in.

But two large men in black coats suddenly marched up with guns drawn. Big black pistols. Jake's gut tightened at the sight. He and Dieter had been blindsided. These guys must have come around from the rear of the house. They must be the punks who clobbered Abel Bauer, Jake thought.

"What do you want us to do with these two, Gerd?" one of the men asked the owner. "Lock them up?"

The man gazed at Jake and Dieter a moment, pondering, and then said, "No, of course not, Ritter.

These men have made a mistake, that's all. Let them go."

Looking at Dieter, he said, "I do not believe that you have a warrant or that your badge is genuine. Just shove off and forget you were ever here. If I hear from you again you will not be so lucky as you were today."

"When you hear from me again, you and these two will be put under arrest," Dieter said.

"Ha, you're too old to be a cop anyway."

"They don't retire the old ones when they're strong and tough," Dieter snapped back. "All right, we will go, but you have not heard the last of us."

As they left, Jake looked back at the gunmen and said, "Better luck next time, *Arschlochen.*" He cocked his thumb and pointed an index finger at them like a gun. It was poor cover for defeat.

When he drove away, Dieter said, "I hope I can get Stumm to raid that place. After he hears what happened, he'll have to."

"For sure," Jake replied. "Churchill's in there! Damn, we were just a few yards away from him. I wonder who that guy was. They called him Gerd, did you notice? He's a pal of Ernst Diels, I guess. "

Now that his home was known, Gerd Honaker knew he would have to act fast. Get his prisoner over to the remains of the Hyperion Theatre. Tonight! Late tonight while the city slept.

* * *

Back at his house, Dieter called Chief Stumm's office, but he wasn't in. "Tell him to call me as soon as he gets back. It is very important," he said. "I have some new evidence for him."

It was lunch time. As she was setting the table, Anna said to Jake, "A message was just delivered for you."

"A message for me?" Jake asked in surprise. "Here?"

"Yes, I will go and get it."

Who could be sending me a message here? I haven't told Colonel Freeborn or anyone else where I'm staying, have I?

Anna returned and handed him a small white envelope.

Jake tore it open and pulled out a piece of paper. Typed words read,

If you want the man you seek, come to the Oberbaum Bridge, West Berlin side, tonight at 8. Be alone and unarmed. Bring money. He will be delivered to you.

Jake sank onto a chair, stunned. The Oberbaum Bridge was one of the east-west checkpoints. Where in hell had that message come from? he asked himself. How could it possibly have come *here*? He chewed on his lower lip. Thought about his conversations with Emma Beck and carpenter Ekhard but reached no conclusions.

What followed was a long and stressful afternoon. Ilse wasn't there. She had gone off to see Leni Riefenstahl again. Anna wasn't there either. Maybe she'd gone off with Ilse.

"They want me to buy Churchill back," Jake said. "Or maybe it's a trap. Or maybe the owner got cold feet and gave it up . . . Naw, I don't really believe that. Be too much to hope for."

"Perhaps you should just ignore the note and stay away from the bridge," said Trudi, sitting nearby.

"If it turned out to be my only chance of saving Churchill," Jake replied, "I could never forgive myself if he turns up dead . . . or never turns up at all."

"This is quite possibly a trap," Dieter said. "If you decide to go, we must be very careful. I would go with you, and with an armed policeman. We will be nearby in the shadows when you go in. If something goes wrong we will rush in and take care of it."

"I hope so."

When Chief Stumm called back that afternoon, Dieter told him, "Never mind, Johannes. My mistake. There's been a new development."

In the end, Jake realized with terrible clarity that, if there was any chance at all to get Churchill, he had to go. It was his duty. He would accept Dieter's offer of backup.

His thoughts turned to Ilse. He hoped she knew what she was doing, but he trusted his clever daughter.

After dark, Dieter drove Jake to the Oberbaum Bridge. A cop named Berndt sat in back, armed and off duty.

Traffic was light. They passed small houses and shops close to the River Spree. Jake sat wrapped in anxiety. Who could have written that message? Would Churchill really be there?

The bridge appeared. The stately brick towers of the old edifice stood high and foreboding in the gloom. Butterflies swirled in Jake's gut.

Dieter parked the car along the street just to the south of the bridge. A few streetlights spilled cones of light on the pavement, but it was mostly dark. "Berndt and I will be in the shadows just short of the bridge," Dieter said. "We will keep you in sight. Are you ready?"

"Here goes nothing," Jake said with false bravado. It was hard to keep his knees steady as he got out. He glanced back at Dieter and Berndt, then turned and walked slowly forward and neared the bridge. It was a clear but chilly night. Just before stepping onto the platform, he caught sight of Venus shining brightly in the west. As a kid, Jake had called it the Evening Star before learning it was actually a planet.

He sees the checkpoint several yards ahead. A wooden barrier blocks the way. GIs and Soviet soldiers are milling around up there under some lights.

Jake draws closer, one small, fearful step at a time. He puts a hand in an empty coat pocket and wishes there was a gun in there. He recalls the time he'd shot a German soldier during the Battle of the Bulge who'd been wearing a stolen U.S. uniform, trying to misdirect American patrols. Jake shoves that from his mind and keeps walking.

Ahead, he catches sight of three men standing in a scrap of darkness this side of the checkpoint, near a small steel stairway leading down to a lower level. One of them is a little stooped and leaning on a cane. Is it Winston Churchill? The other two stand upright.

Well, here goes.

Jake takes two more steps.

The two men spring forward and grab hold of him. Strong arms encase him like vise grips. Haul him off his feet. "Dieter!" Jake shouts. "Dieter."

As they drag him down the stairway, he catches a glimpse of the man with the cane. A young face. It's not Churchill.

"Hey, what!" a voice yells out. One of the border guards.

Jake is lugged helplessly along the lower landing. His heart thuds like a pile-driver. These guys are brawny and strong. He hears rapid footsteps clattering up above. Dieter and Berndt. Border guards. Too late. Too late.

THIRTY-THREE

Dieter drove away, swearing. "*Verdammt,* we should have been closer."

"How could we have been closer without being seen?" Berndt said. "We had the best position we could have managed."

"My poor, poor nephew," Dieter uttered, and cursed some more. "*Sohn einer Hündin.*" Son of a bitch. He wouldn't be able to get the police to raid that house till morning. He knew Chief Stumm wouldn't be in his office at this hour and he didn't know where the man lived or his home phone number.

"Maybe the Americans will do something," Berndt said. "You told that sergeant what this was about."

"Berndt, he would need to talk to his superior, who would then kick it up to higher authority. It would take hours or longer. I don't see how the occupation force could move fast on this." Dieter slapped the steering wheel. "I'm so mad at myself. It's a *verdammt* foul-up.

We'll just have to get Stumm to raid that house in the morning. That could be too late."

"Maybe they took your nephew to someplace else instead of that house."

"Damn, Berndt, I wish you hadn't said *that*."

Dieter was driving too fast.

Taking stock of this stranger, the moon-faced elderly man in the rumpled gray suit asked, "Do you happen to have a cigar? I haven't had one for days."

Jake had been shoved into a sorry-looking room with a steel door and a bricked-up window. The man he saw was unmistakably Winston Churchill. The care-worn face, the hunched back and shoulders, the wooden cane.

"No sir, I'm afraid I don't." Jake had a purplish bruise below the right eye. His face hurt. He'd been roughed up quite a bit on the way here.

"Who are you, young man?" Churchill asked. He had gotten up from the bed, but now sat back down on it. He wore a white shirt with an undone bow tie. His large head was nearly bald, with only a straggle of wispy gray hair above the ears. A dark overcoat lay beside him on the bed.

"Mr. Churchill, my name is Jake Weaver. I'm an American. I was asked by a retired MI6 man to come to Berlin and see if I could find you. I'm sorry I had to find you in this way, locked here in this crummy room." Jake knew the crummy room was at Number 14

Spreewegstrasse. He'd recognized the house when he was hauled here.

"Not a palace, is it?" Churchill said. "Who is this MI6 man?"

"Colonel Harold Freeborn, sir."

"I know of Freeborn. He has done some extraordinary work for us. And why did he turn to you on this?"

"I did some things for him during the war. I—"

"Oh yes, you're the chap who found Wernher von Braun, aren't you? I was told about that. I approved the George Cross for you. You are quite an extraordinary fellow."

"Not really," Jake said. "How have they been treating you, sir? Are you all right?"

"As all right as one could expect at my age. I'm not exactly fit as a fiddle. Twice a day they bring me some wretched food and some water. I could make use of a good single-malt whisky about now, but alas, no such luck. The captors say very little to me, although when I was first placed in here, a most agitated bloke snarled at me and said, 'You will see Sikorski's ghost.' Haven't the foggiest what he meant by that. They allowed me to have some paper, though, so I have been sitting here for days working on my memoirs. Little else to do." He gestured toward a scribbled-on pad of paper on the bed. "I shall now include you in them."

"No need to do that, sir," Jake said, and sat on a small wooden chair, the only furniture in the room besides the single bed, a small table, and a foul-smelling chamber pot. He wondered if this would be the last day of his life. He'd been in some bad fixes before, but this one was right up there. Probably the worst. The people who'd kidnapped Mr. Churchill couldn't afford to leave witnesses. Jake desperately hoped he could get back to Valerie, but what were the odds? His life was in forfeit.

Trying to hide those fears, he asked Churchill, "How was it that you were captured, sir?"

"I was just leaving the office of East Berlin Mayor Ulbricht when I was accosted by two men with a gun at my back and before long I found myself here. Rather rude of them. Most inconvenient."

"That's a hell of an understatement, sir."

"I always say there's no point in melodrama. I had come here secretly from Bonn to meet with Soviet Premier Malenkov. I had hoped we could find some common ground and agree to ease the tensions in this so-called Cold War. I also wanted to urge him to allow Deputy Nazi Fuehrer Rudolf Hess to be released from prison. The old fellow is feeble and suffering from dementia. Let the harmless bloke live out his last days in freedom.

"Our clandestine meeting was to take place in the East Berlin city hall. But first I met with the mayor of West Berlin, Mr. Schreiber, to pay her majesty's respects. After that, I went to Mr. Ulbricht's office, as had been quietly arranged, to meet with Chairman Malenkov. I had yet another reason to see Ulbricht. Perhaps I'll go into that later. To my chagrin, he had heard from Moscow that Malenkov was detained and could not come. You can imagine my disappointment. It was upon leaving Ulbricht's that these two rapscallions waylaid me. I say, that's quite a nasty bruise on your face, Mr. Weaver. You were beaten?"

"Yes, a bit." Jake reached up and touched the painful spot. "Somehow these people found out I was looking for you. They arranged a rendezvous, but it turned out to be a trap. Two men, probably the same ones who rousted you, used me for punching-bag practice on the way here."

He must have hit back. Jake realized that two of his knuckles were cut and red. They stung.

"Rum go, that, the rogues," Churchill was saying.

There was just a touch of the World War II sprightliness left in this man. He looked depleted, but Jake recognized his need to talk, a need for human contact. The man had been alone here for days.

"Didn't you also meet with a neurologist, a Dr. Diels?" he asked.

"So you discovered that? Yes, you see, I have a slight infirmity and I hoped he could help. He ran a test or two but I was apprehended before he could get back to me."

"Diels is a bad guy, sir. He's working with the East Germans. He's the one who tipped off these people."

"I see. You've done some good spadework, Weaver. I must admit I did not take a liking to the fellow. How is it that these people got on to you?"

"My uncle is a retired Berlin police officer. He's been helping me. He knows about this place. We were able to find this address. Somehow these people found out we were looking for you."

"Damned bad luck, that."

Jake recalled telling that carpenter, Ekhard, that he was staying with Dieter. Stupid mistake. Damn his big mouth. Ekhard was pissed off that Jake bullied him into giving up this address, so he ratted to these guys, and that's how they knew where to send that message about the bridge.

"And how do you come to have an uncle in Berlin?" Churchill asked.

Jake explained that he was a second generation German-American, a son of Berlin parents, and that his father was the uncle's brother. He added that he'd used his language skills to help President Roosevelt and MI6 during the war.

"You've led quite an extraordinary life," Churchill said. Extraordinary seemed to be the man's favorite word.

Jake said he was pretty sure his Uncle Dieter would have the cops raid the place and get them out.

"I sincerely hope so, Weaver. You believe, then, that we shall leave this place alive?"

Jake wasn't at all sure about that, but he said, "Yes, I think so."

"I do hope you are right. I have a score to settle in Parliament with Clement Attlee."

They passed the time conversing, each one bringing the other up to date on themselves. Jake told of his newspaper days and his new job in television. "My life hasn't been as exceptional as yours, sir. All the great things you've done in two wars and afterward."

"Actually, four wars," Churchill said. He went on to tell about the Boer Wars. "I was captured in the second Boer War, you know, imprisoned at Pretoria. I was a fledgling correspondent for the *Daily Mail* at the time. The Boers ambushed the train I was on. I managed to scale a wall and make my escape. Unfortunately there is no wall to climb here," he said, looking around the drab room. "I crossed more than a hundred miles until at last I reached the Second Royal Dragoons. I did not walk that entire distance. I must confess that I hitched a ride on a freight train part of the way. Hobo'd, I believe is your American term."

He rambled on, telling about the amphibious Gallipoli fiasco in the Great War when he was First Lord of the Admiralty. "It was a good plan, but too slow in forming. It leaked out, and the blasted Turks were waiting in force. After that, I served in the lines with the Royal Scots Fusiliers in France." To Jake, this was like a verbal reading of his memoirs.

"When I was called back again to lead the Admiralty in the early days of the Second World War, the signal to the fleet simply said, 'Winston is back!' How that pleased me."

"What was your best moment during the war?" Jake asked.

Churchill thought a moment and then said, "When we defeated Rommel in the Western Desert and saved Egypt, I should say. Erwin Rommel was an able tactician and a worthy opponent. And, well . . ."

Jake sensed that he wanted to say more about Rommel, but then decided not to. "And what was your worst times during the war?" he asked.

"The fall of Singapore was a total shock. Quite devastating. I could not believe the fortress was so poorly defended. But no, the U-boat menace was the worst, definitely the U-boat menace. It was touch and go for two years as to whether sufficient supplies could get through to keep us in the fight. A desperate time. Breaking their naval codes and improved technology at last swung the Battle of the Atlantic in our favor. It was a near thing."

Jake knew Churchill had resisted the Normandy invasion as long as he could. Like many Britons, he'd harbored bitter memories of the terrible losses they suffered in France in the first war. Instead, he had argued for an advance up through Italy and the Balkans, what he called "the soft underbelly of Europe," to take Germany from the south. This roundabout and mountainous route was flatly vetoed by the Americans, who considered it folly, and insisted on the shortest possible route to Berlin across northern France. Jake kept quiet about all that, though.

He thought that U.S. forces had fought more effectively after D-Day than had the British, who took weeks to capture their first objective, the French town of Caen. He kept mum about that, too.

Churchill said, "My mother, you know, was American. Had it been the other way round, har har, I should have been a Yank too. Wouldn't that have been something?"

Jake found all this exceedingly strange, even creepy, talking about this great man's life experiences when both were captives and their lives probably on the line.

"You have found out a great deal, Weaver," Churchill said, "but here is one thing you do not know. May as well tell you now. I had another agenda item for Chairman Malenkov, a warning. Before his death, Stalin had been cozying up to Egypt's strongman, Mohamed Naguib, and was starting to give him military and technical aid. This could embolden Egypt, with Russian help, to try and nationalize the Suez Canal, and we just couldn't have that.

"I had planned to tell Malenkov in the strongest of terms, 'Hands off the canal. I don't care if you do have the atomic bomb, the Suez Canal is British, always has been, and always will be.' A shot across the bow is called for with Mr. Malenkov. We do not fear the Russian bear."

Tough talk, but Jake wasn't buying it. There was no way Britain could fight Russia, even over the precious canal. There were two great powers in the world today, and the UK wasn't one of them. This was no longer their finest hour.

Sir Winston seemed to realize that too. "Sadly, the greatness of Britain," he said, "is fading. The 19th century was ours, but the 20th belongs to America. I pray you and your country will treat it well."

"I spoke before of my respect for Erwin Rommel,"

he went on. "To his credit, Rommel became, you know, involved in the plot against Hitler, and sad to say it cost the good man his life. When our SAS force raided his headquarters in North Africa in 1942, they pinched a silver-framed photograph of his wife Lucia. I approved of the raid of course but not of that act of looting. I'm sure the picture meant a lot to him. So, in Chancellor Adenauer's office in Bonn the other day, I met with Rommel's son, Manfred. This was before I came here. I expressed my condolences, gave him the picture, and asked him to give it to his mother. Young Manfred was most grateful."

"I'm sure he was, sir. That was a fine gesture."

"I hope I'm not boring you, Weaver. I do bang on."

"Not at all," Jake said. "I'm enjoying this conversation. Now, you mentioned that you had another reason for seeing Ulbricht. What was that, sir?"

"You see, during the war, Walter Ulbricht was one of the German officers on Jersey, one of our Channel Islands they occupied. He and his henchmen did some foul looting there. The curator of the little museum in the capital of St. Helier said that Ulbricht stole the Coutances Cross from there."

"The Coutances Cross?"

"Right, this item was brought to the island by a Norman bishop in the 12th century. It is a small gold cross with diamonds inlaid at each of its four corners. It became the island's most cherished icon, as important to them as the Stone of Scone is to us. Their crown jewel, so to speak. Would you care to see it?"

"Sure, but how could I possibly see it?"

Churchill bent down, pulled up his right pant leg, removed a garter, and extracted something from beneath his black stocking. He held up the Coutances Cross for Jake to see.

He was awestruck. The exquisite little cross was no more than three inches by four. The small diamonds sparkled, the gold gleamed.

"I shall see that this is returned to its rightful place in the museum."

"That's great, sir, but how the devil—"

"The English bobbies on Jersey took note of Ulbricht's sexual tendencies. He preferred sleeping with men, you see, and this information made its way to MI6."

"But how—"

"Being homosexual is a crime in East Germany, as it is in Britain, a felony offense. I simply told Ulbricht that I would inform the Berlin press of his proclivities, unless—"

"A beautiful bit of blackmail, sir."

"Quite. I'm rather proud of it myself." With that, Sir Winston returned the cross to its hiding place and pulled his pant leg back down, saying, "I should like to keep this secret."

"My lips are sealed and my pen sheathed."

"I knew I could count on you, Weaver."

And now Churchill seemed to wilt. At first, his voice had sounded strong, much like his stirring wartime speeches. But it had grown weaker as the conversations wore on. His broad shoulders sagged. Fatigue lined his cherubic face. He yawned and said, "It is growing late. Perhaps we should try to get some sleep."

"It's a small bed, sir. I'll sleep on the floor."

This whole experience would have been extraordinary— that word again—for Jake, if he hadn't been a prisoner in this damned room. A condemned prisoner, no doubt. He lay down on the wool carpet using his coat as a pillow. His face still ached from the punches he'd taken.

What a story I could write and produce about this man's life. If I can live to do it. But this Gerd person can't possibly allow Churchill and me to go free. My body could be floating in the River Havel before Dieter and the cops crash this place—if they ever do.

Churchill ambled to the wall switch, saying, "I shall turn off . . ."

The sentence was cut off by a sudden flinging open of the door. The same two thugs who'd captured Jake barged in, one of them brandishing a pistol. The other one carried some lengths of rope and scraps of black cloth in his hands. This was the punk who'd punched Jake in the face and gut an hour or two ago. Oh, how he wanted to rush this guy and pound him with his flashing fists. But the other man had his gun leveled at Jake's heart.

A third person entered. It was the man who'd answered the door when he and Dieter had come to this house, the man called Gerd. He also carried a pistol.

"The next scene in our little drama will take place at a different venue," he said. "My friends will bind your hands and blindfold your faces. Cooperate with them as they do this. If you give them any trouble they will shoot you down here and now."

Jake wanted to give him the old left hook. But knew that would be the last thing he'd ever do in his life.

THIRTY-FOUR

Twenty minutes later.

They had taken a short ride. Jake had no idea what kind of car it was, but it sounded and smelled like a diesel.

"We will go down some steps now," said one of the goons. "Be careful."

Someone clutched Jake by the arm as he began to descend. Blindly. Whatever was underfoot felt solid, more like concrete than wood. He stumbled on something—a crack? a hole?—but the hand that gripped him kept him from falling. Level ground at last beneath his feet. He had reached the bottom. The bottom of what?

The air smelled dusty and musty, like the cellar at his cousin's place at Opelousas.

"All right, untie them," said the voice of the man called Gerd. First, the ropes binding Jake's hands came off. His wrists hurt, felt raw. He began rubbing them.

He thought about throwing a blind punch but what good would that do? Get him shot, probably.

Then the blindfold came off. He could barely see. But soon a flashlight beam revealed Winston Churchill a few feet away, being freed from his bindings. The beam swept widely around.

This seemed to be a large room of some kind. Jake caught a glimpse of several odd things. A couple of steamer trunks. Clothing in various colors, on pegs and hangers, and draped over chairs. Was that a fake tree? A suit of armor? Dust lay thick over everything. There were cobwebs. It was cold. Broken chunks of concrete on a hard floor.

"This will be your new home . . . for a short while," said the Gerd person. Sounding almost gleeful. "Seat yourselves before we depart."

The light shone on one of the trunks. Churchill slowly lowered his tired old body and sat on it. The light swung to another. To Jake, it looked much like the footlocker he'd had in the Navy. He perched himself on it.

"*Auf weidersehen*," said the voice. "Dresden! Hamburg! My father!" The words spat out hatefully. The light swung about on the stairsteps as the three captors climbed out. What sounded like a heavy door clanged shut.

Total blackness now. Despair clutching at Jake like a predator. He rubbed his wrists again. His eyes gradually began to adjust, and soon he could see small strips of moonlight seeping in overhead from jagged holes in whatever kind of ceiling this was.

Suddenly, a small flickering light off to his left. Winston Churchill had struck a match. In that dim, sputtering light, Jake made out some queer objects. What looked like a scenic backdrop, a mountain with clouds hanging above it. That suit of armor again. Baskets. Chairs. Milk cans. All manner of costumes. Scraps of concrete and masonry rubble on the floor. Load-bearing pillars, some of them bent and leaning, doing damn little bearing. It was a big underground room falling to pieces. "I think we find ourselves in the remains of a theater prop room," Churchill said.

The match was burning low. Churchill shook it out and again only faint strips of moonlight remained. "How many matches do you have?" Jake asked.

"I've a small packet, perhaps eight or nine remaining. I prefer lighting a cigar with a wooden match. Never much fancied those petrol lighters."

"Light another one if you would, sir, and let's set one of these dresses on fire. That'll give us enough light to do something I have in mind."

Churchill did that. As the match flared up, Jake went over to a wall hook. Stumbled on a broken chunk of concrete, but managed to keep his balance. Removed a long, filmy dress that hung there. "Here, let's set this thing ablaze." He held it by the neck as the prime minister leaned down and applied his match to the blue hemline.

When the dress was well ignited, Jake dropped it to the floor, picked up a caneback chair and with one giant swing, whacked it against a rough concrete wall.

"What the devil are you doing, Weaver?"

"Making a weapon, sir."

Jake bashed the chair again and it shattered. He picked up two of its legs and handed one to Churchill. "We have a couple of billy clubs now, sir."

"Rather like a bobby's nightstick," Churchill said. "Thank you for thinking of this. A damn shame I lost my umbrella somewhere along the way tonight. Shameful, an Englishman without his umbrella."

"Sir, when these guys come back, they'll have guns but we'll at least have surprise on our side—and these." *If* they come back, it will be to kill us, Jake was thinking but didn't say. "At least we can go down fighting."

"Right you are, by jove," Churchill said.

The dress consumed, the fire flickered out and blackness filled the room again, along with the smell of burnt fabric.

"Well, I'm gonna lie down now," Jake said, "catch a little shuteye if I can, but keep a hand on my billy club."

"I shall do the same, removing my coat to use as a pillow." The voice of the British lion was weak, softened by what must be extreme fatigue. That saddened Jake as he lay down on the hard floor, weapon at his side.

He'd slept without a mattress on hard surfaces before, once in Nazi Germany and a few times in the Navy. It was uncomfortable as hell but he could manage. He hoped there weren't any rats in here. So far he hadn't heard any sounds of little scuffling feet.

Dark recollections swirled. The time when thugs

ambushed him in Washington and broke his foot. He had just come from meeting with Congressman John F. Kennedy at the Capitol.

Finding Rolf Becker here in 1942 and the bitter disillusionment of discovering that his "friend" was actually an enemy agent. Becker's attempt to kill him. The fear that gripped him in Nazi Germany that same year when he realized he'd gone too far in interviewing Reichsmarshal Hermann Goering.

Apprehended outside Joseph Goebbels' home in Lanke and thrown into a Gestapo prison. The electric wires clipped to his arms and genitals. The searing pain jolting every nerve in his body when the sadist turned on the juice. Jake thought he was going to die that day. Was he thinking the same thing now?

Even though he was lying close to a famous man of history, he never felt more alone.

THIRTY-FIVE

DAY SIX

Jake actually did doze a little, but fitfully.

His subconscious took him to Espiritu Santo Island in the New Hebrides. A U.S. military hospital, late summer 1942. He'd just met a young Marine Corps sergeant who'd been wounded on Guadalcanal. Was interviewing the lanky young man from the Midwest, whose name was Kenny Nielsen.

Kenny was eager to be released so he could go back to "the canal" and rejoin his platoon mates. They were like family to him. He'd felt like a deserter not being with them as they fought the Japanese.

A pretty nurse named Claudia Chase came by a couple of times during the interview. She seemed very protective of her patient, the small touches of his arm, the tender glances she couldn't quite manage to hide. She urged Jake not to tire Kenny out.

Jake had no idea that Claudia and the Marine would later be married and that he and Valerie would become close friends of the young couple. That he and

Kenny one day would coauthor a book about the war. Life could be full of surprises like that.

In his half-sleep, Jake wondered if life would have any more surprises for him. Or even if he would have much more life at all.

Sounds from up above startled him. He was instantly awake. Frightened and stiff all over, he took hold of that chair leg.

Flashlight beams began bouncing down the stairs. Many footsteps. The treads creaking. Jake couldn't tell how many people were behind those descending lights. Those two punks, at least.

The beams of light reached ground level. One of them approached him. It drew right up in front of him, blinding his eyes. This was it. Showtime.

He swung the chair leg against the intruder's ankle. The person fell and tumbled onto him. The flashlight crashed to the floor. Who the hell was lying on top of him? Another light swung toward him.

"*Vati*, is that you? Are you all right?" Hearing his daughter call him daddy in this room, in this place, at this time, was the most surprising sound Jake had ever heard.

Another flashlight beam was swinging around. He heard Anna's voice saying, "Here is Herr Churchill."

Jake found himself lying beneath Gretchen Siedler. She had a pistol in her hand.

Face to face with Jake, her weight pressing on him,

Gretchen said in a husky, teasing voice, "Hello, you. My, Jake, it's been years since we've been in this position, hasn't it?" She gave a mischievous grin and a ripple of laughter, and then slowly pushed herself up.

Embarrassed—at some other time this would be funny—Jake got to his feet. Separated now from Gretchen, he uttered, "My God, Ilse!" His daughter rushed up and hugged him.

"What are you, female commandos?" Jake said. "How did you—"

"We figured it out, the four of us." Ilse said. "Leni Riefenstahl is here too."

"Come on, we must leave quickly. This is technically East Berlin. We have some ground to cover." Jake didn't recognize the voice. It must be Leni Riefenstahl.

THIRTY-SIX

Earlier, Ilse and the other three had come to Honaker's house at Number 14 Spreewegstrasse. Her father had given her the address.

Honaker had peered through the peephole in the front door and recognized the woman standing there. He opened the door and said, "Why, it's Leni Riefenstahl, isn't it?" He had spoken with the cinematographer before, the last time being at the after-party of a film opening. "To what do I owe the—"

Leni took a step forward, shoved him back into the room and was followed inside by three strange women, all carrying guns. "What?" he blurted, but Leni shoved him again, hard, on his chest.

"Take a seat, Herr Playwright," she demanded. "We're going to have a little conversation." Stunned, Honaker sank onto a chair.

Gretchen Siedler said, "Ilse and Anna, check the rest of the house, see if anyone else is here, and find that room. Be careful."

"*Was im Hölle*," Honaker blurted, but Gretchen cut him off, shouting, "Shut up!"

Anna returned, saying, "No one else is here."

Then Ilse came in. "I found the room. It's a damn cell, is what it is. I never saw a door like that in a bedroom before. But the room is empty. No one is there." Her face seemed to sag with dread. She knew her father might be dead. And Winston Churchill as well.

Ilse plopped down on the sofa beside Leni Riefenstahl, facing Honaker. "Where are they?" Ilse demanded. Honaker returned her stare and said nothing.

"Where are they?" she repeated, louder this time. "The two men you had here."

"But I've been told to shut up," Honaker said with a small grin.

Ilse had fired a pistol before, years ago at a private gun club with her father, so she knew how. The Swiss Pistole 49 in her hand was loaded—she'd made sure of that. Safety off. She raised the weapon and leveled it at Honaker. "Where *are* they?"

Honaker remained mute.

Ilse fired. At the wall. Less than two feet above Honaker's head. The loudness shocked her. Sound rattled off the walls like thunder. A jagged black hole appeared in the plaster behind him.

Honaker was shaken. Eyes wide, face trembling. But still said nothing.

"Where are they?" Ilse said, more calmly now. "Last chance." She tried for an evil smile. Seconds passed.

Now she aimed the pistol toward his face, from which no words came.

The second shot seemed even louder. The table lamp beside Honaker's head exploded. Shards of glass showered his face and hair. A sharp smell of cordite filled the room.

That did it. Whimpering like a baby, he opened up. A small red cut on his cheek, he said all right and told them about the Hyperion Theatre.

"Well done, Ilse," Leni said. "I know that theater."

The women found some towels and ripped them into strips. Before tying Honaker's hands and feet, Gretchen ordered him to take off his shoes, stockings, and pants.

Leaving Honaker in his underwear, skinny white legs shivering, bound hand and foot, the four of them departed. Leni drove, saying she knew where the damaged old Hyperion Theatre was. A block away from the house, Gretchen, in the front passenger seat, lowered her window and tossed the pants and shoes into the street.

I didn't know if I could do that, Ilse told herself. Fire those shots toward that swine. Surprised myself. Did I really do that? She wondered, would Nellie Bly have shot that pig in the face after she'd gotten the name from him?

The six of them clambered up the stairs and reached ground level amid the ruins of the theater. They began hiking to the west across the construction site, passing trucks and bulldozers silent in the light of a half moon. West Berlin was just yards ahead.

A sudden flashlight beam caught them and a man in some kind of uniform approached out of the gloom. "What are you doing here?" he demanded.

Leni Riefenstahl countered, "Who are you?"

"My name is Schmidt, private security for Munger Construction. This site is off limits. You are trespassing. Who are you people?"

"We're a theatrical group," Leni told the watchman. "We perform humorous skits and impressions at the cabaret just over there. It's convenient for us to take this shortcut rather than go around to the checkpoint, which is such a nuisance, more than half a mile away. You needn't worry, we never steal anything."

Schmidt panned his light slowly across their faces. He lingered longer on Churchill's than any of the others, apparently puzzled. Leni felt she had to say something.

"This is Freddi," she said. "He does an impersonation of Winston Churchill that is quite good."

"He does, does he? I see some resemblance, but he can't be very good. He is too short . . . All right then, you may pass but do not come through here again. Demolition will commence tomorrow."

"*Danke. Guten Abend*," Leni said and the six scurried off.

"Not very good?" Churchill scoffed.

* * *

Soon they were all back in the house on Spreewegstrasse. Gerd Honaker was still there, a pathetic,
sniveling, lost man. Goosebumps on his thin, bare legs.
If he'd been able to free himself from his bindings, he
would have had to go outside in his underwear. He
hadn't been able to.

"What an extraordinary rescue," Churchill was
saying. "Who are you splendid valkyries?"

Gretchen made the introductions and Churchill
said, "Good show, ladies. You are heroines, which is a
lovely thing for women to be."

Everyone took seats, Jake beside his daughter on
the sofa, Gretchen on the other side of him. The others
occupied chairs.

"You charging in there with your flashlights and
pistols was the greatest thing ever," Jake exclaimed,
putting an arm around his daughter. "You were like the
cavalry riding to the rescue. How in the world did you
find us?"

Ilse explained. "When Dieter came home last night,
he told us what happened at the bridge. The poor man
felt terribly guilty. You'd given me this address, so
Anna and I hurried to Leni's flat and we got organized.
We came here, found this man and forced him to tell us
about the theater."

She didn't mention that she'd fired two shots toward
the man, but Jake saw the shattered lamp and bullet
hole in the wall. He was proud of this daughter who
wanted to be the next Nellie Bly.

"That's an ugly bruise on your face, *Vati*," Ilse

said, reaching up and touching it. "What happened?"

"I got roughed up a bit. Nothing to worry about. It's happened before."

"You women were splendid," Churchill said. "I would tip my hat to you, had I a hat to tip. Lost it during the past two days." He held up the first two fingers of his right hand in the "V for Victory" sign he'd made famous during the war. Then he caught sight of a pack of cigarettes and a cigar box on the coffee table. He eagerly opened the box, extracted a cigar, and began peeling away the wrapper. "It's been a long time. Do you ladies mind if I smoke?"

Leni laughed and said, "Puff away to your heart's content, Sir Winston."

Churchill pulled his matchbox from a pocket and fired up the cigar. "Ah, at last," he uttered. He rounded his lips and blew a perfect smoke ring.

Leni Riefenstahl, pointing at Gerd Honaker, said, "We will turn this *Bösewicht* over to the police."

"Not if—" the man began, but Leni cut him off. "I told you to shut up." She looked at the others and said, "Let's throw this guy in that cell he has. Why didn't we do that before?"

"Didn't think of it," Ilse said. "We were in such a rush to get to that theater. We'll take care of it right now, though. Come on, *Vati*." She and Jake untied Honaker's feet but not his hands, and hauled him, stumbling, to that altered bedroom, embarrassed with his skinny white legs exposed. "*Bitte, nein*," he begged.

"You were happy enough to throw me in here,"

Jake said. "Now it's your turn, you pathetic *Arschloch*."
He gave Honaker a hard shove, closed the door, and
turned the lock.

As they were disposing of Honaker, Gretchen went
to the kitchen, found the coffee and brewed some.
Minutes later, she was back in the front room with six
cups on a tray. More morning light now came from the
window.

With the group reassembled, Ilse described how the
four women had met—twice—and decided what they
must do.

"Extraordinary," Churchill said, puffing away at his
stogie. "I will see that you receive some suitable awards
for this exemplary feat . . . but quietly. I do not wish
it known what has happened to me here. Pray, do not
inform the press. I shall be most happy to leave this
city."

Ilse stood and gave Anna a big hug. "You were
wonderful," she said. "The Bund would be proud."

At length, they heard cars squealing up in front.
Soon the door flew open and Dieter burst in with Chief
Stumm and four policemen at his heels. They held
weapons at port arms, pistols and a submachine gun.
Dieter's mouth fell open at what he saw.

"Welcome to the party, gentlemen," Leni Riefenstahl
said. "You're a little late."

"*Ach du lieber*," said Stumm.

THIRTY-SEVEN

Churchill was introduced to Dieter and Stumm. He shook their hands, said some kind words, and then used Honaker's phone to call the Hotel Kempinski. He told bodyguard Seaton where he was and told him to get here.

While this was going on, Gretchen took Jake's hand and pulled him into another room. "I still love you," she said, and kissed him.

"Keep it a secret, okay?" Jake replied. "Thanks for helping us, Tapestry."

After Chief Stumm phoned to summon a couple of detectives to the house, Jake told Churchill he should keep out of sight when they arrived. He knew how leaky police departments could be. "Stay in the bathroom or something, sir. They mustn't see you."

"Exactly what I had in mind," Churchill said.

Jake cautioned the others not to mention the man, and Stumm concurred.

The detectives arrived. While they were questioning everyone, taking down their statements, Jake drew Ilse aside, gazed into her eyes, and said quietly, "Firing on a human being is a watershed moment in one's life. I know."

"What makes you think I—"

"Come on, *Leibchen,* I see the bullet holes in the wall there, and I smelled some gunshot residue when you brought your hand up to my face. What went through your mind before you fired?"

Ilse paused, then: "Honestly nothing, *Vati.* I didn't hesitate for a second. Your life was on the line. I could never live with myself if I couldn't find out where you were."

Jake was left speechless. He hoped she could see in his eyes how moved he was. Eyes that were forming tears. He wrapped her in his arms. She laid her head on his shoulder.

Later, after another round of congratulations, Winston Churchill was flown to London from Tempelhof Airport on a British jet, which he quietly boarded at night, across the field from the terminal. He had a daughter's birthday to get to.

Before leaving, he shook Jake's hand goodbye. "You're a grand fellow, Weaver," he said. "Marvelous that we met." Jake had shaken hands with a number of prominent people, including Franklin Roosevelt, Harry Truman, William Randolph Hearst, Wernher von

Braun, and Congressman Jack Kennedy. But shaking Churchill's affected him more than any of the others. He was humbled.

Sir Winston Churchill would retire two years later at eighty-one years of age and turn to painting and writing his memoirs.

Gerd Honaker would be convicted of criminal abduction and thrown in prison. So were the two thugs who'd done the kidnapping, with felonious assault added to the charges.

The carpenter Ekhard was fined for building-code violations and altering a residence without a permit.

Chief Stumm said the press would be told none of this. Nonetheless, stories did appear in West Berlin newspapers saying that Churchill had been in town. The police indeed had leaks. The British government flatly denied the tale, the London press called it poppycock, and before long it was largely forgotten.

Ernst Diels abandoned his practice and disappeared in East Germany.

Churchill's bodyguard was reassigned to the city parks department shortly after arriving in London.

The Coutances Cross mysteriously reappeared in the museum at St. Helier. This became known as the Miracle of Jersey.

Jake planned to write and produce a story for CBS about Adolf Hitler's half-brother Alois, who still ran a small bar and café in West Berlin.

Nikita Khrushchev replaced Georgi Malenkov as party chairman in Moscow.

* * *

Jake and Ilse had a final meal at Dieter's with Trudi and his uncle. Anna served a rich cabbage soup, spinach salad, and beef tenderloin. Dieter asked her to join them at table rather than eat in the kitchen as she usually did.

"What a fascinating few days this has been," Trudi said, putting down her fork. "All this has done you some good Dieter, *mein Schatzi*. You look years younger." Jake caught a twinkle in her eye. Did she sneak a glance toward their bedroom or was that just his imagination?

"This is a wonderful meal, Anna," Jake said. "Best I've had in a long time." The young woman blushed and nodded her thanks.

"I will write to you, Anna," Ilse said over their dessert: banana cream pie with a dollop of vanilla ice cream. Then she made an announcement. "I'm going to stay on for another week at Leni Riefenstahl's. She has offered me a small part in the film she's producing at the zoo. I've decided to take it."

Acting? Jake's daughter never failed to surprise him. "Being an actress for a while and then writing about it is the kind of thing Nellie Bly would do," he said.

"Exactly," Ilse replied. "If I don't have a job when I get back, I'll find another. *The Daily Mirror* has made an offer or two."

Jake recalled having similar thoughts when Bill Hearst Jr. had taken over the *Herald-Express*. Quite a girl! He would fly home alone then.

While Ilse helped Anna clear the dishes, Jake called Lufthansa and booked a seat. He then asked his uncle if he could make a transatlantic call. "By all means," Dieter replied with a fatherly smile.

It was 2 a.m. when the phone rang in Valerie's bedroom. "Oh oh, I hope this isn't bad news," she grumbled as she reached for the receiver.

It was good news instead, very good news.

■

CPSIA information can be obtained
at www.ICGtesting.com
Printed in the USA
FSHW011639121020
74673FS